WINGS OF FIRE

OF

FIRE

FORGE YOUR DRAGON WORLD

WINGS OF FIRE

OF
FIRE

FORGE YOUR DRAGON WORLD

BY TUI T. SUTHERLAND

ART BY MIKE HOLMES
COLOR BY MAARTA LAIHO

AN IMPRINT OF
SCHOLASTIC

With special thanks to Sarah Evans

Library of Congress Cataloging-in-Publication Data available

ISBN 978-1-338-63477-8

10 9 8 7 6 5 4 3 2 1   21 22 23 24 25

Printed in China
First edition, May 2021
Edited by Amanda Maciel
Coloring by Maarta Laiho
Lettering by John Green and E.K. Weaver
Creative Director: Phil Falco
Publisher: David Saylor

Dear Writers, Artists, and Story Creators of All Sorts,

When I started writing the Wings of Fire series, I had lots of clear images in my mind: the mountain cave where Clay and his friends grew up; the SeaWing scales that glowed on Tsunami's wings; the SkyWing arena where the dragonets are held prisoner; Sunny's cheerful smile and Glory's colorful camouflage. And like Starflight, I wanted to capture all those ideas in a book so it could come alive in readers' imaginations.

Then we started adapting *The Dragonet Prophecy* into a graphic novel and — WOW! Suddenly the pictures from my brain had taken on a new shape, and in full color! From the SeaWing Deep Palace to the Rainforest Kingdom, the world of Pyrrhia was both exactly how I imagined it and completely new. Barry Deutsch helped shape my chapters into panels and scenes, and then, between Mike Holmes's captivating art and Maarta Laiho's colors, it felt like my dragons were flying off the page!

Creating a story in words and pictures is the closest we humans get to real magic, and I'm so excited to share some of my process with you here! In this guidebook, you'll get to bring your own ideas to life. And I can't wait for you to share your brilliance with me and the world!

Let your imagination soar!

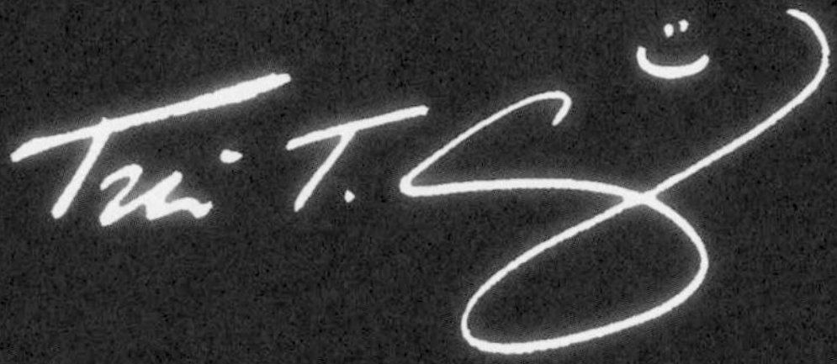

Tui T. Sutherland

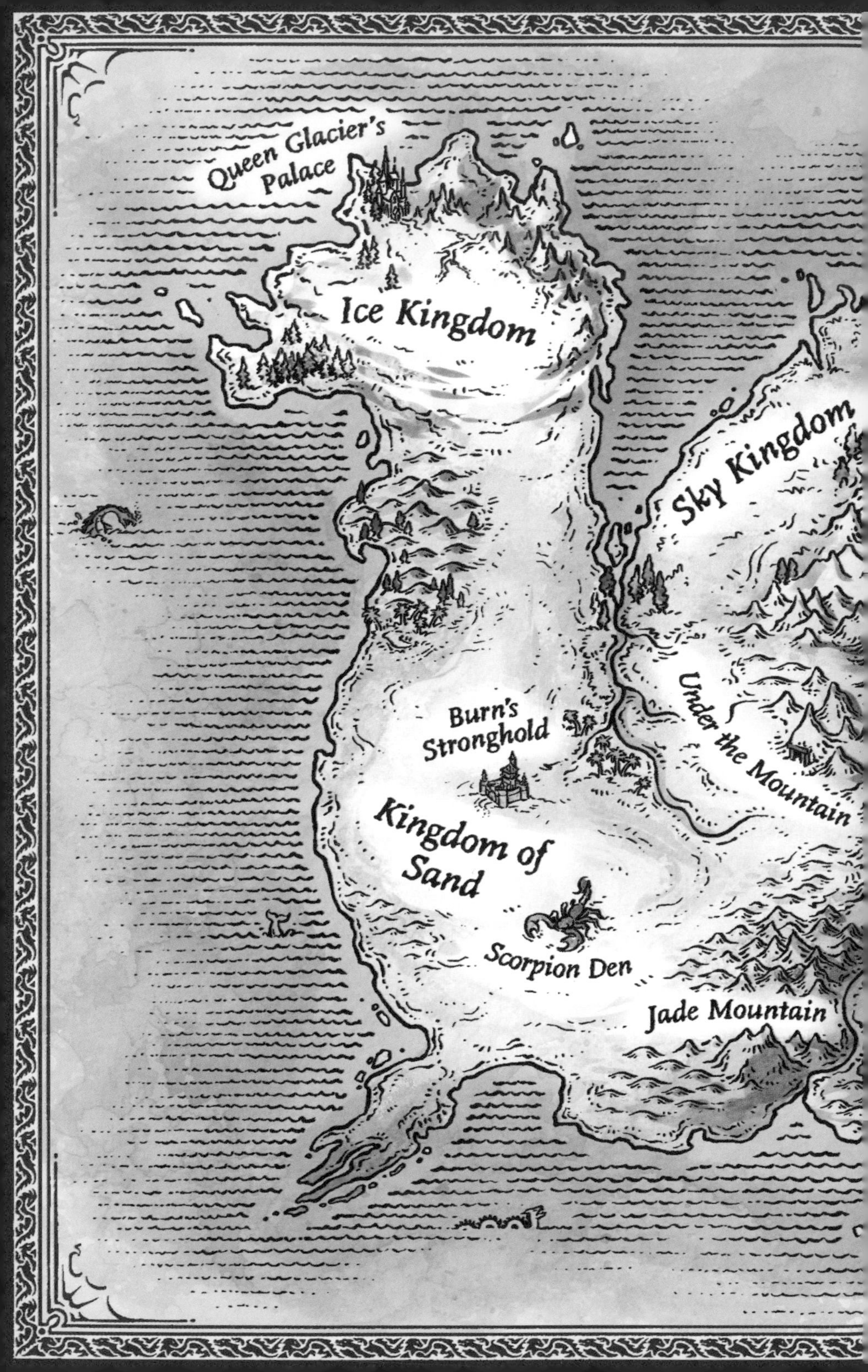

Queen Glacier's Palace
Ice Kingdom
Sky Kingdom
Under the Mountain
Burn's Stronghold
Kingdom of Sand
Scorpion Den
Jade Mountain

TABLE of C

CHAPTER 1: STORY SPARKS

CHAPTER 2: DRAGON HATCHINGS

ONTENTS

CHAPTER 3: WORLDBUILDING

CHAPTER 4: FLYING STARTS

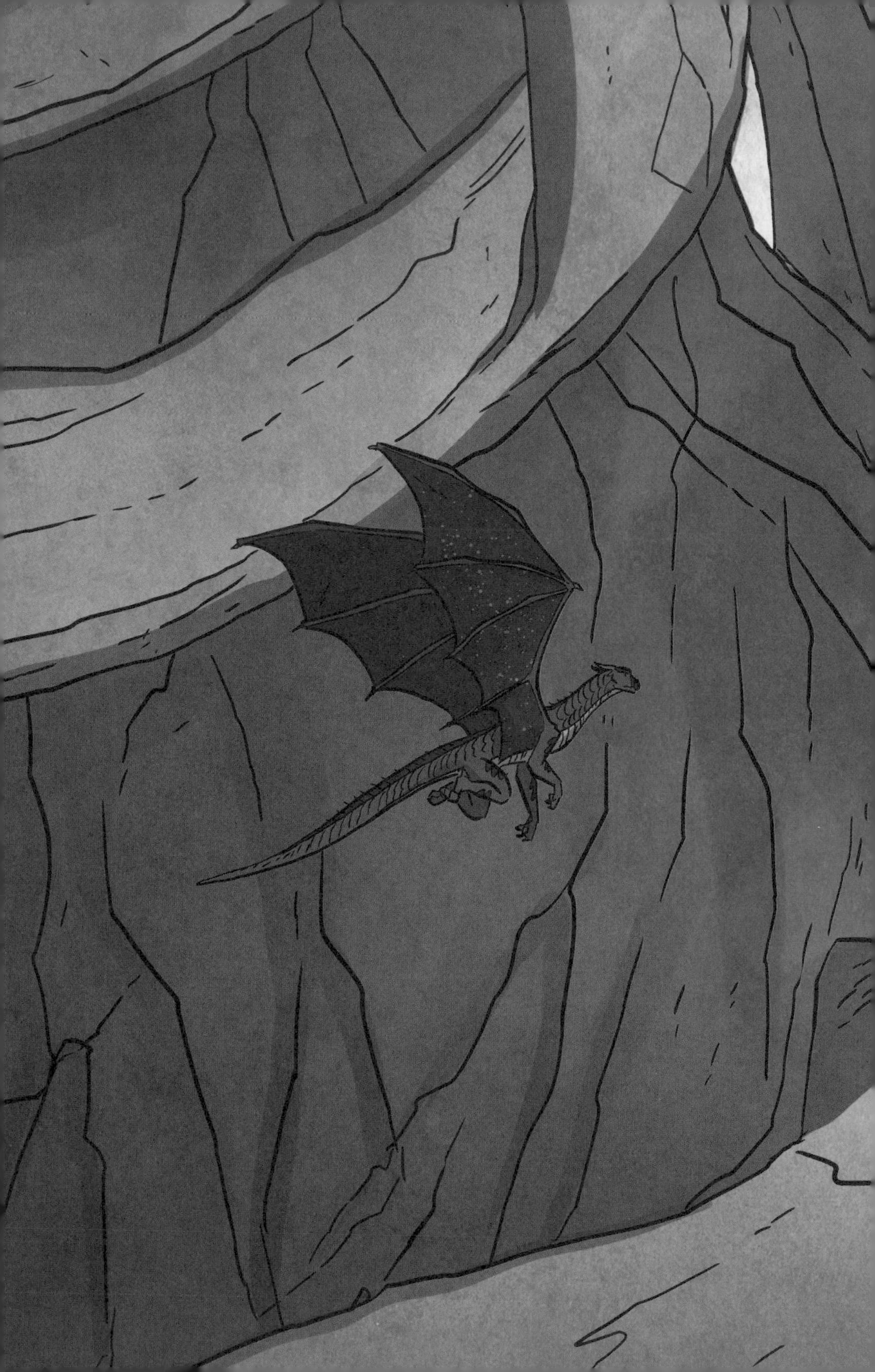

CHAPTER 1
STORY SPARKS

GET STARTED

People love to ask authors where they find their ideas. The truth is, every writer has a unique answer to that question. Sometimes a character idea sparks the beginning of a story. Or you might overhear a conversation while walking down the street one day, and suddenly inspiration strikes. Stories are everywhere — if you know where to look . . .

THE MISSING PRINCESS AGAIN?
HELP ME WITH THE HARD PARTS?
"MAD WITH GRIEF, THE QUEEN EXCLAIMED, MY EGG! OH, WHO HAS STOLEN MY SEA-BLUE EGG?"
NO, SKIP TO THE END.
"HER JOYOUS PARENTS THREW A FEAST FOR THE WHOLE KINGDOM. THEY DINED ON OYSTERS AND TURTLES AND WHALES..."
AND THEY ALL LIVED HAPPILY EVER AFTER... TOGETHER.

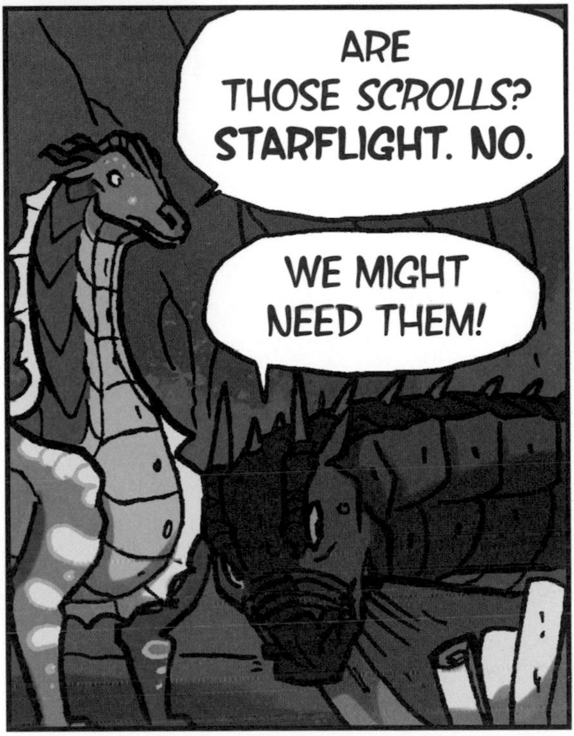
ARE THOSE *SCROLLS*? STARFLIGHT. NO.
WE MIGHT NEED THEM!

In this book, you'll gather story ideas, create awesome dragon characters, imagine new worlds, and decide how YOU want to tell your story. Do you love to write? Do you love to draw? Do you want to write a novel or create your own graphic novel? This is the book for you!

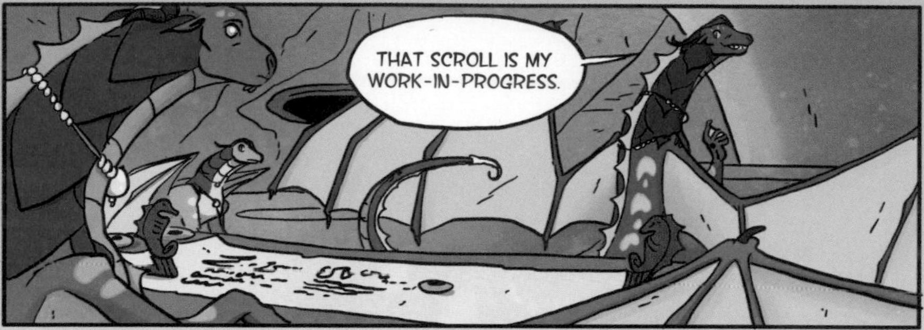
THAT SCROLL IS MY WORK-IN-PROGRESS.

FIND YOUR IDEA

Maybe you want to write a story, but you don't have a BIG IDEA yet. That's okay! Not every idea has to be a big one. And some small ideas can grow and grow.

One way to come up with ideas is to keep a scroll — er, journal — of your own life. You don't have to write pages and pages (but you can if you want to!).

Here's a place to practice. Write down at
least five things you did this week.

- MY cusens
  came.
- ~~I came~~
- I Bowncst
  on a Giyent
  tnampleh.

DRAGONS ARE PEOPLE, TOO

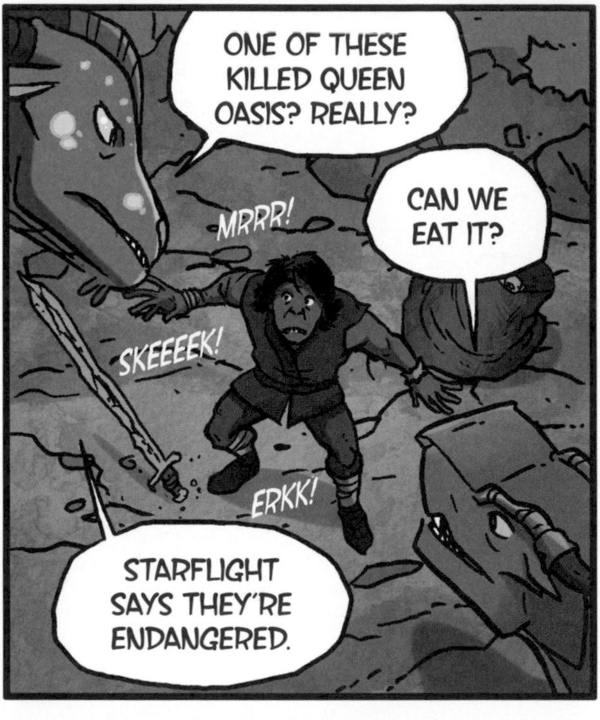
ONE OF THESE KILLED QUEEN OASIS? REALLY?
CAN WE EAT IT?
MRRR!
SKEEEEK!
ERKK!
STARFLIGHT SAYS THEY'RE ENDANGERED.

You might be thinking, *But this is a story about dragons! Their lives are much more exciting than mine*. Well, yes, dragons can fly, and some of them can breathe fire, or breathe underwater, or poison enemies with their tails or their magical death spit . . .

But they also have some of the same challenges we scavengers face. They fight with their family or friends, they have teachers who want them to study hard, they have crushes on other dragons, they have to figure out how to end a war because there's this prophecy . . .

STOP MAKING HER MAD!
ME? WHAT DID I DO?
WELL, YOU'RE A HANDSOME IDIOT.
SHE HAS A CRUSH ON YOU.
SHE DOES?
IT'S PRETTY OBVIOUS.

Okay, sometimes they might not be *exactly* the same.

YOU CAN'T BE SEEN WITH US. SHE'LL KILL YOU! YOU HAVE TO HIDE!

WHICH CAME FIRST, THE DRAGON OR THE EGG?

Go back to the list you made of what you did this week. If you're anything like Starflight, your list includes both *what* you did (read scrolls) and *who* you saw or talked to this week (Sunny and Morrowseer). You might even have said *where* you were (probably in a cave).

Some writers like to start with the *what* of the story: What is happening? Is there a war going on? Is there a prophecy to end it?

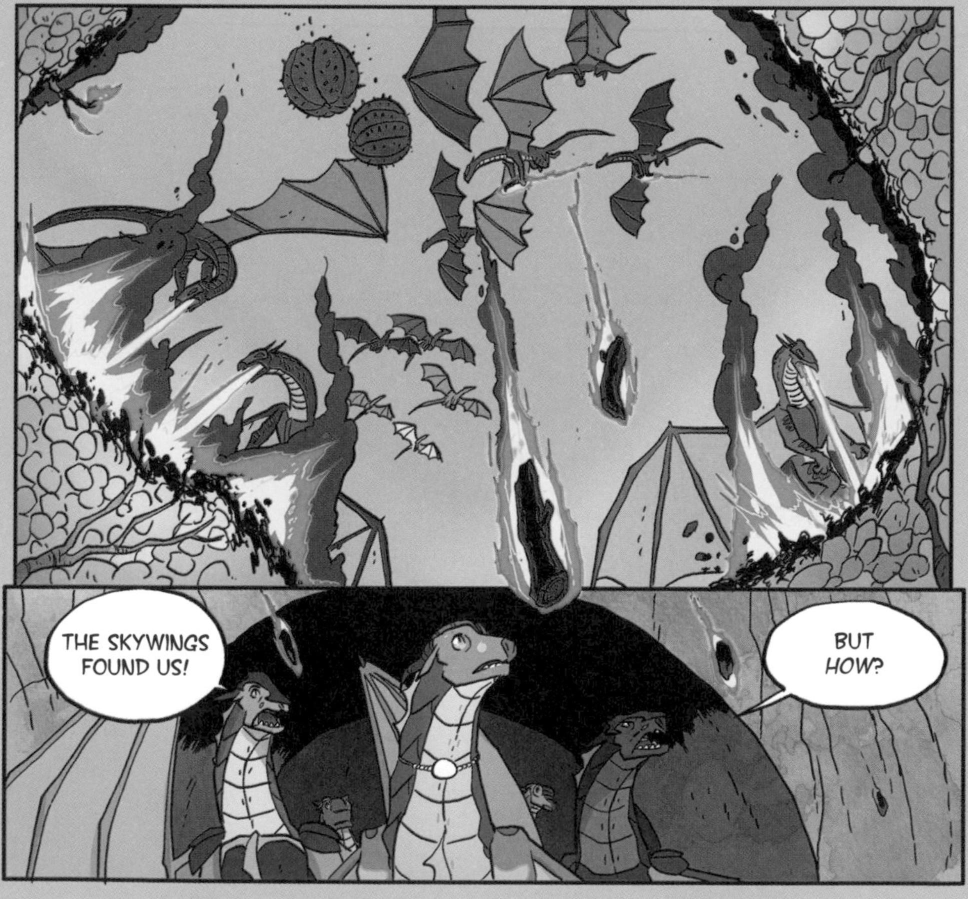
THE SKYWINGS FOUND US!
BUT HOW?

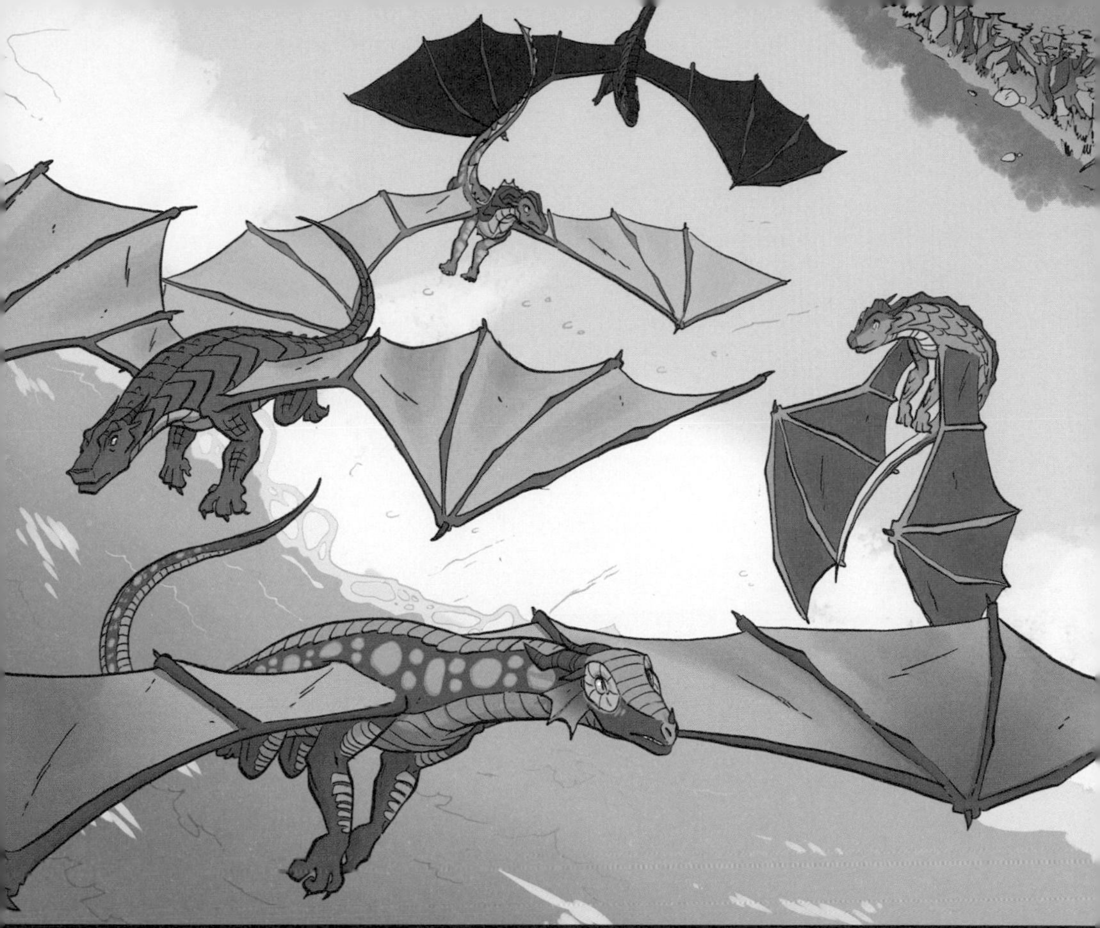

Others like to start with the *who*: Who are your characters? Are your dragons warm and protective like Clay? Optimistic and excitable like Sunny? Sarcastic and tough like Glory? Smart and nervous like Starflight? Or strong and impulsive like Tsunami?

And other writers like to start with the *where*: Where does the story take place? Are there different environments, like the Kingdom of the Sea and the Rainforest Kingdom? Is there magic? What kind of history does this world have?

WHERE WILL YOUR STORY START?

If you like to start with the *what*, keep reading Chapter 1! If you like to start with the *who,* skip to Chapter 2, and if you like to start with the *where,* go to Chapter 3 — but be sure to come back!

WHAT? Pick a conflict
Imagine a fight scene between two dragons who used to be friends!

WHO? Create a character

Name:

Age:

Pronouns:

Tribe:

Size:

Scale coloring:

Powers:

Home:

Family/friends:

Personality:

WHERE? Build a world

Continent name:

Environment(s):

Residents:

Magic:

History:

CHOOSE YOUR CONFLICT

The *what* at the heart of your story is called the conflict. Here are some Wings of Fire examples!

Burn
Blister
Blaze

DRAGON VS. DRAGON: The three SandWing princesses all want to be queen, and they've pulled most of the other kingdoms into their war.

FIGHT!
I'M TRYING! MAYBE IF WE COULD STOP AND TALK—

DRAGON VS. SELF: Clay wants to be a good fighter, like his guardians think he should be and like the prophecy requires, but his heart isn't in it.

DRAGON VS. NATURE: Escaping from a mountain via an underground river is hard, even if you CAN hold your breath for a very long time!

GASP! GASP! GAAAAAAASP!
I'LL JUST LIE HERE AND DIE FOR A WHILE.
EVERY PART OF ME HURTS.

WE HAVE TO PICK ONE, RIGHT? WHEN WE FULFILL THE PROPHECY? WHO DO WE CHOOSE WHEN THEY'RE ALL SO TERRIBLE?
I DON'T KNOW.

DRAGON VS. FATE: The prophecy says the dragonets of destiny are supposed to choose the next SandWing queen and end the war . . . but what if they want to make their own decisions about the future?

AS THE NIGHTWINGS FORETOLD . . .

The NightWing prophecy tells the story of one of the main conflicts in Wings of Fire:

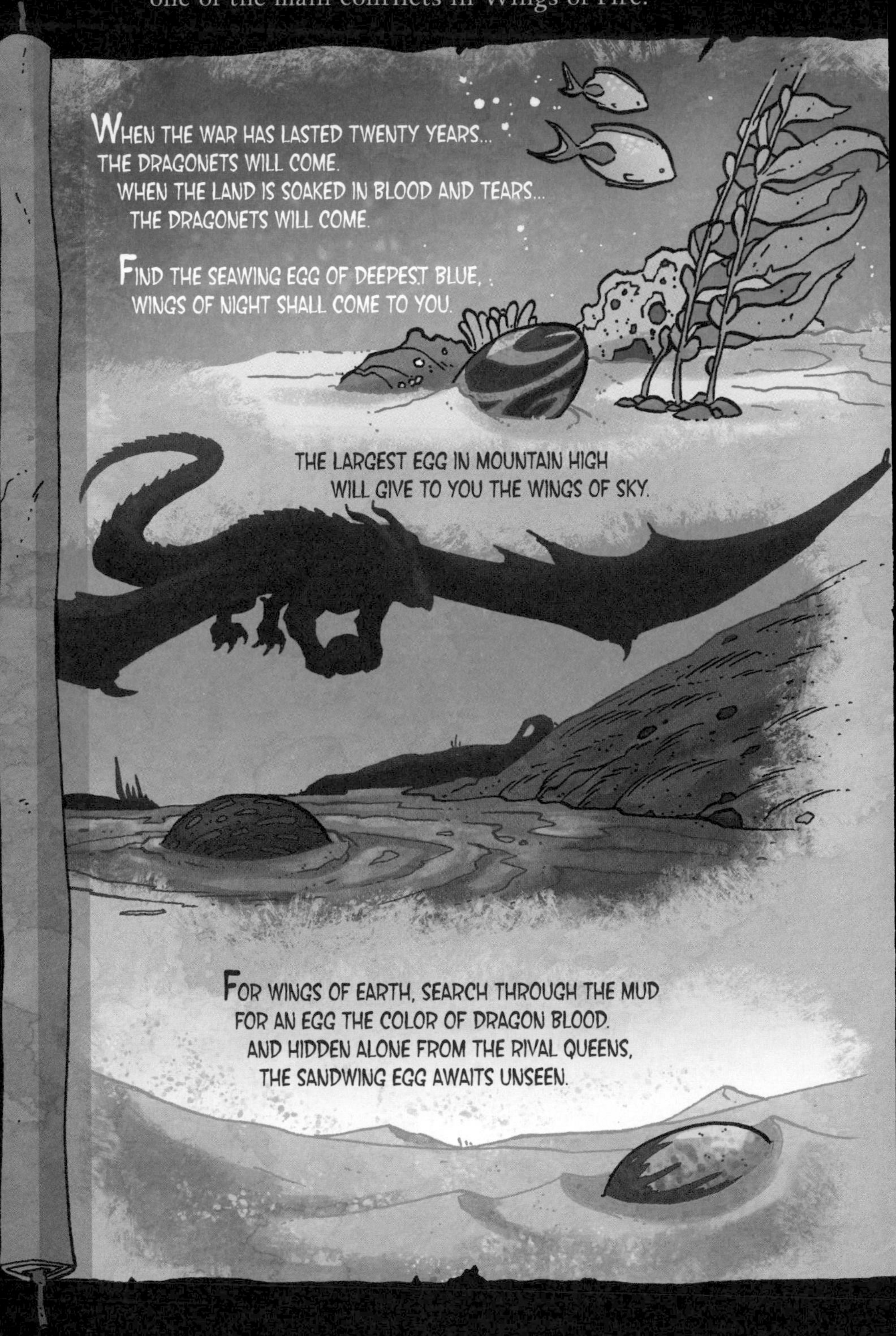

WHEN THE WAR HAS LASTED TWENTY YEARS...
THE DRAGONETS WILL COME.
WHEN THE LAND IS SOAKED IN BLOOD AND TEARS...
THE DRAGONETS WILL COME.
FIND THE SEAWING EGG OF DEEPEST BLUE,
WINGS OF NIGHT SHALL COME TO YOU.
THE LARGEST EGG IN MOUNTAIN HIGH
WILL GIVE TO YOU THE WINGS OF SKY.
FOR WINGS OF EARTH, SEARCH THROUGH THE MUD
FOR AN EGG THE COLOR OF DRAGON BLOOD.
AND HIDDEN ALONE FROM THE RIVAL QUEENS,
THE SANDWING EGG AWAITS UNSEEN.

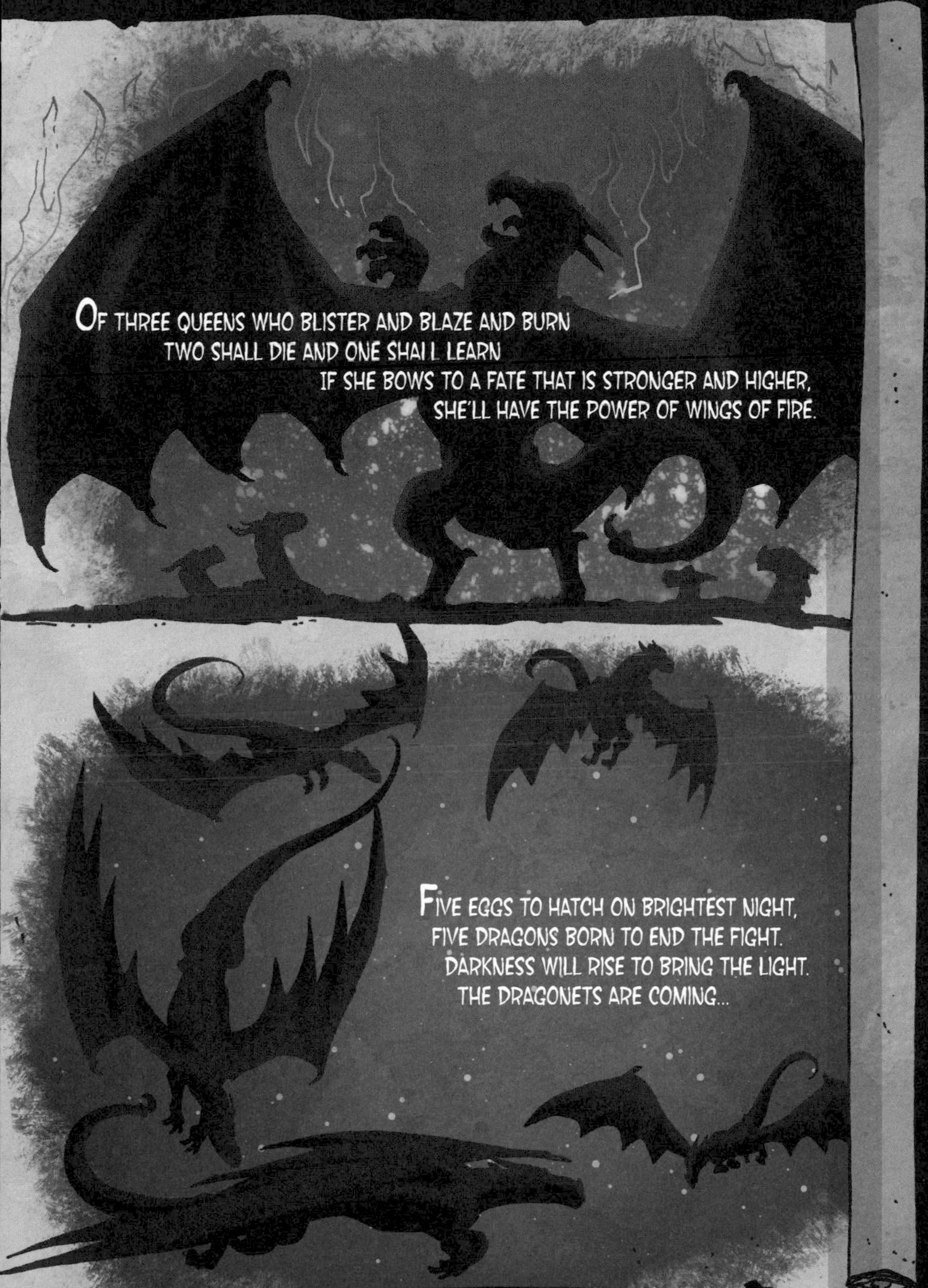
OF THREE QUEENS WHO BLISTER AND BLAZE AND BURN
TWO SHALL DIE AND ONE SHALL LEARN
IF SHE BOWS TO A FATE THAT IS STRONGER AND HIGHER,
SHE'LL HAVE THE POWER OF WINGS OF FIRE.
FIVE EGGS TO HATCH ON BRIGHTEST NIGHT,
FIVE DRAGONS BORN TO END THE FIGHT.
DARKNESS WILL RISE TO BRING THE LIGHT.
THE DRAGONETS ARE COMING...

WRITE A PROPHECY

Not every dragon story needs a prophecy, but telling the future in your story can be fun! It also helps you brainstorm what you want to have happen to your characters.

Here are some tips:

Be specific about a few things
> "Of three queens who blister and blaze
> and burn, two shall die."

Keep some details vague
> "One shall learn if she bows to a fate that
> is stronger and higher, she'll have the
> power of wings of fire."

Try to sound mysterious and poetic
> "And hidden alone from the rival queens,
> the SandWing egg awaits unseen."

WRITE YOUR OWN PROPHECY!

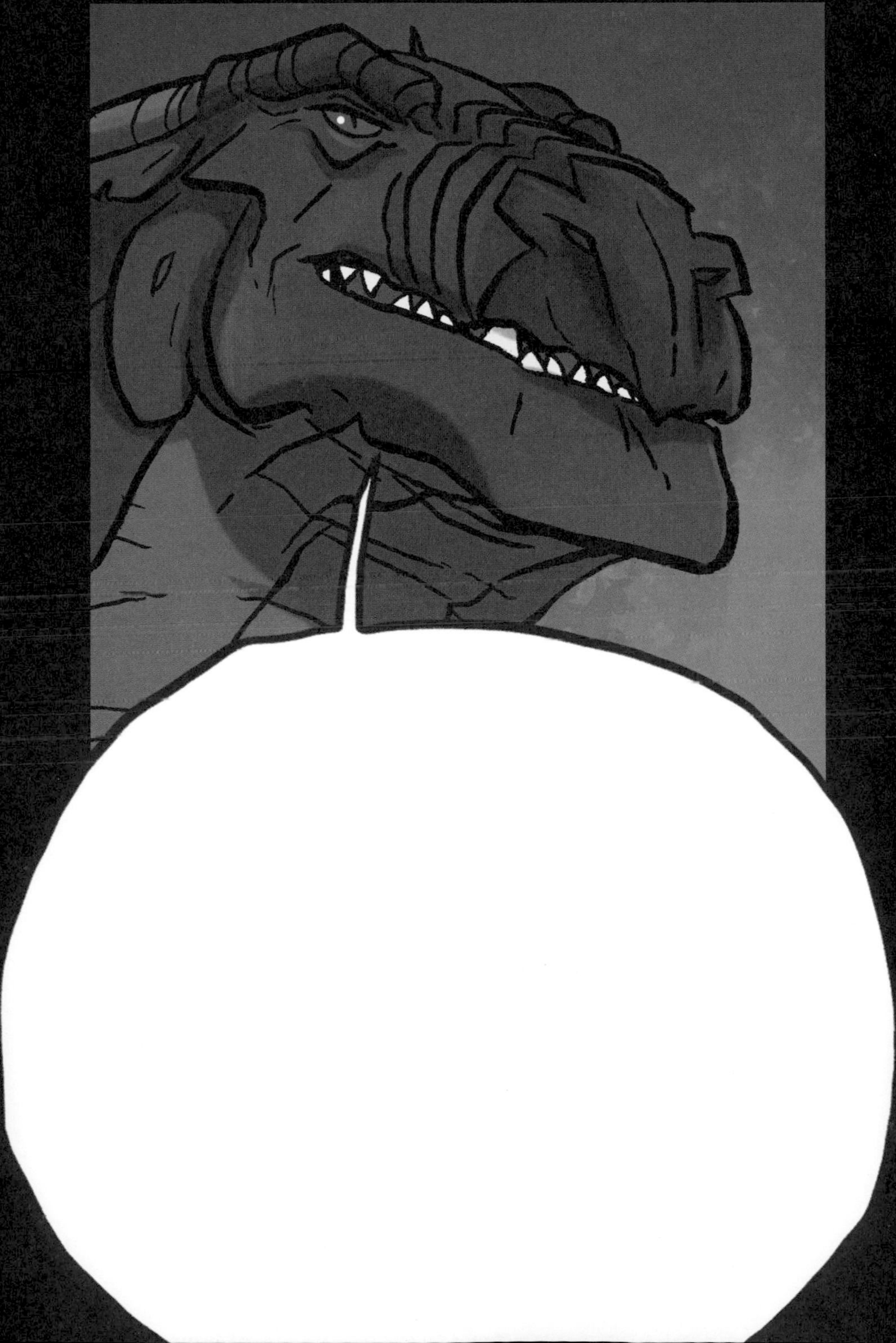

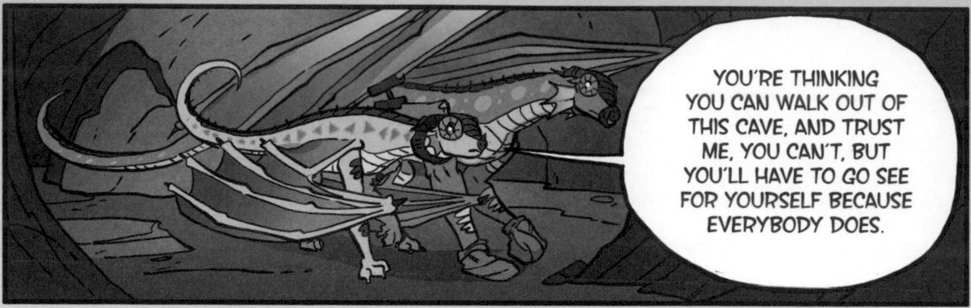
YOU'RE THINKING YOU CAN WALK OUT OF THIS CAVE, AND TRUST ME, YOU CAN'T, BUT YOU'LL HAVE TO GO SEE FOR YOURSELF BECAUSE EVERYBODY DOES.

ESCAPE A TRICKY SITUATION

Whether your dragons are stuck in a cave, surrounded by fire, or high atop a SkyWing prison, there's no doubt they'll have to come up with a clever plan to find their way to freedom.

On these pages, come up with some tight spots your dragons might have to escape . . .

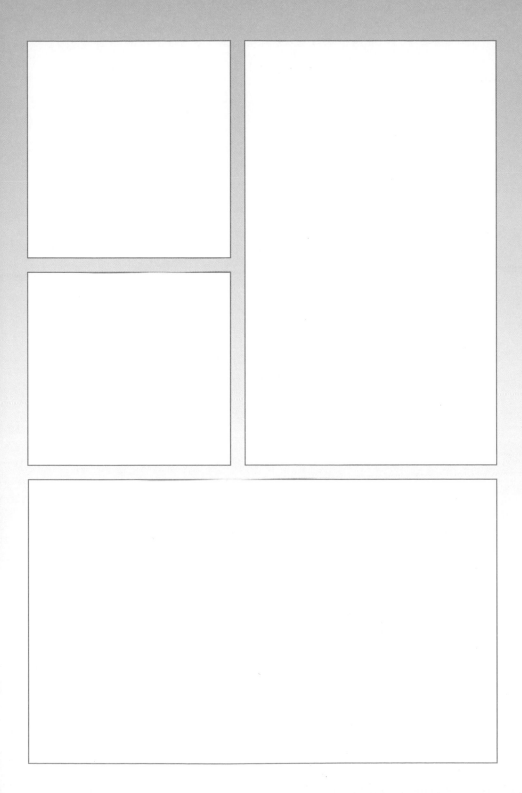

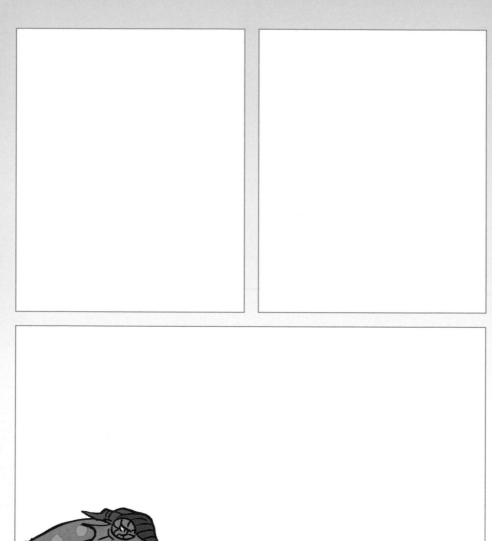

SET OUT ON A QUEST

In Wings of Fire, almost all the dragons are searching for something. The dragonets of destiny want to discover how to end the war — but they also want to find their families. Some dragons want to find treasure — including animus-touched objects that will let them do magic!

What could your dragons be trying to find?

STORY TIPS FROM TUI

Try to write at least one sentence every day!

Think about your characters' biggest problem and how they might solve it by the end of the story.

Make sure you're having fun!

Look for surprising solutions and twists, not just the first or easiest ideas that pop into your head. If you get stuck . . .

- Go for a walk
- Talk to a friend
- Take a break and work on something else

· BLOW SOMETHING UP!

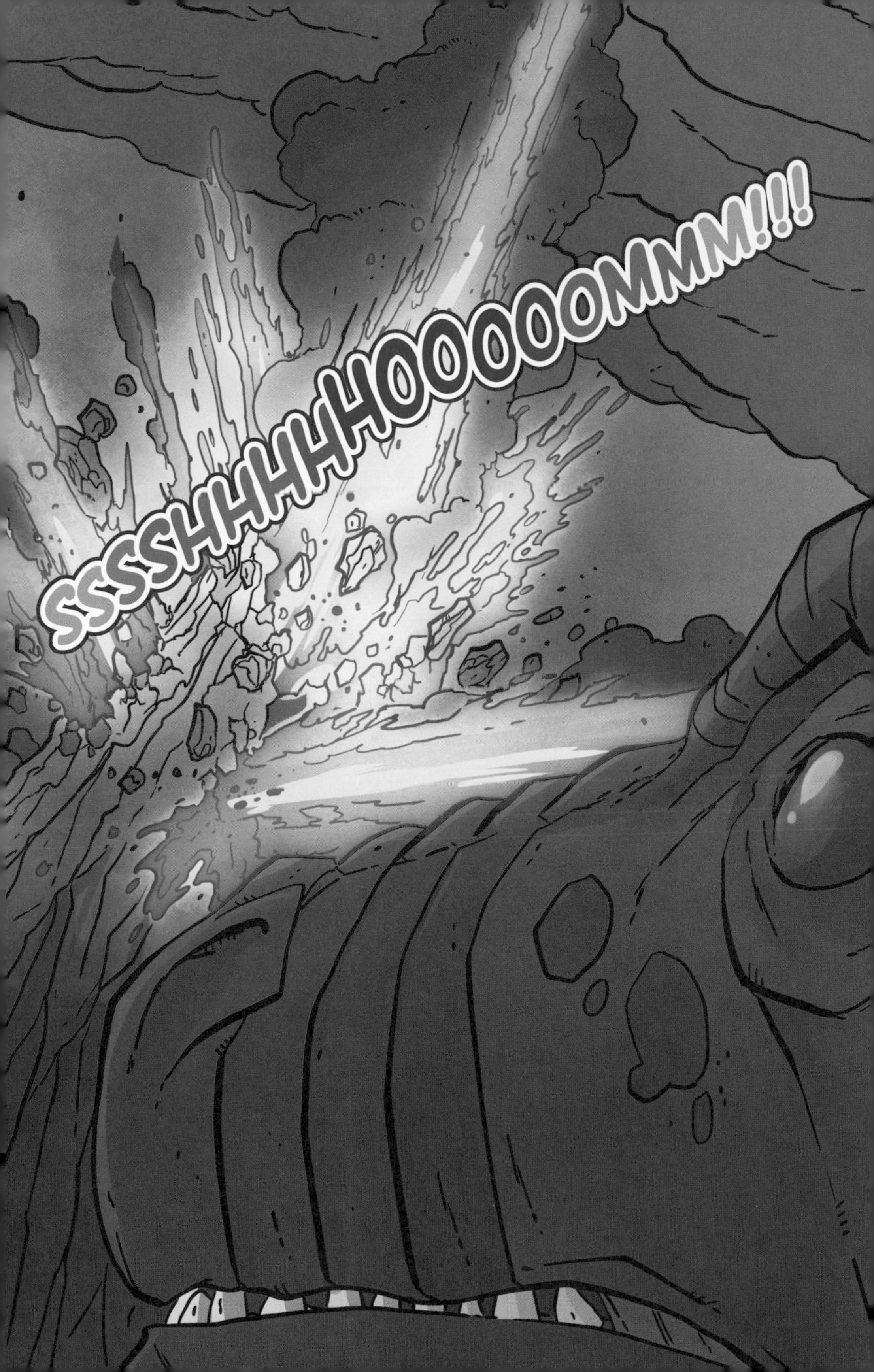
SSSSHHHHHOOOOOOMMMM!!!

STORYSTARTER

Create a scene where your dragon finds something unexpected while flying at night.

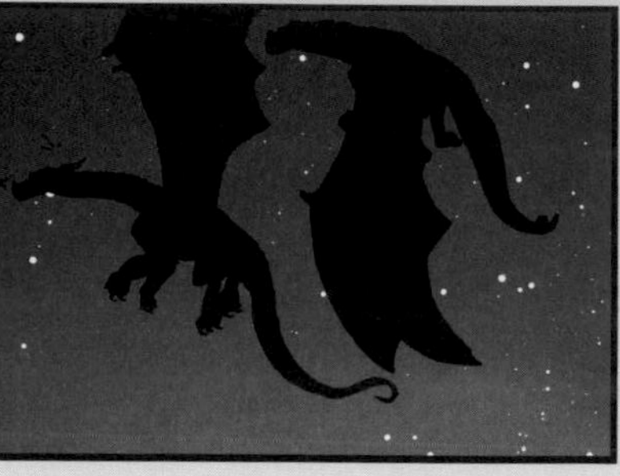

STORYSTARTER

Create a scene where two dragons meet for the first time.

HELLO! I BROUGHT YOU SOMETHING TO EAT.
PLOP!
HI! I'M PERIL. THE QUEEN'S CHAMPION. AREN'T YOU GOING TO EAT? WHAT'S YOUR NAME?
CLAY.
COME ON, YOU HAVE TO EAT.
WHY?
BECAUSE I DON'T WANT YOU TO DIE BEFORE I KILL YOU.

STORYSTARTER

Create a scene where a dragon finds what they've been seeking . . .
but it's not quite what (or who) they thought it would be.

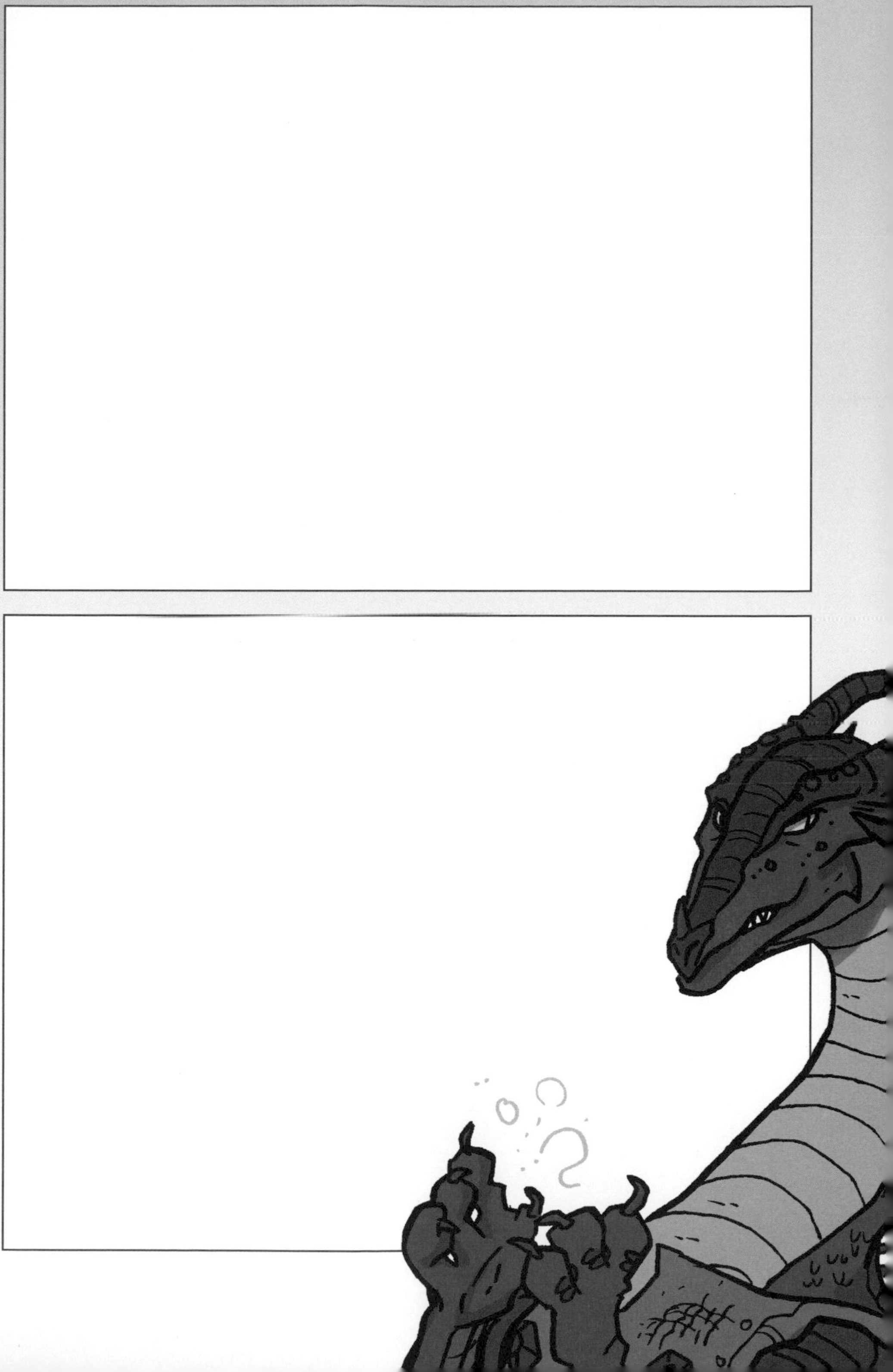

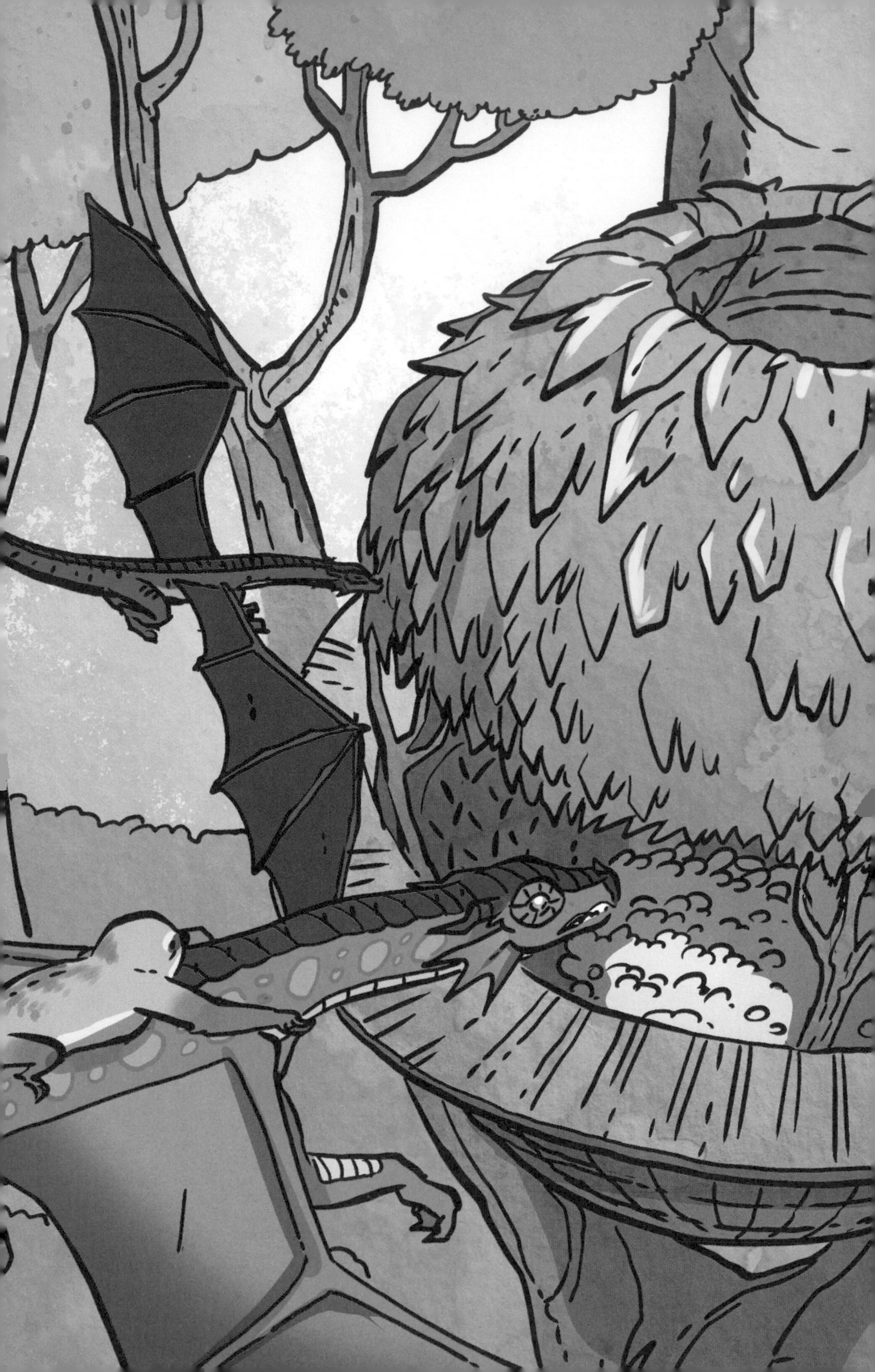

CHAPTER 2

DRAGON HATCHINGS

CHOOSE A NAME

Choosing the right name for your dragon is important. Would Sunny seem quite as bright and bubbly if she were called Quicksand? Peril IS pretty perilous to most dragons! And Deathbringer's name is perfect for an assassin — even one who makes a lot of jokes!

In Pyrrhia, dragons' names are usually related to their tribes. Having a naming theme helps establish who your dragon is and tells us something about the community to which they belong.

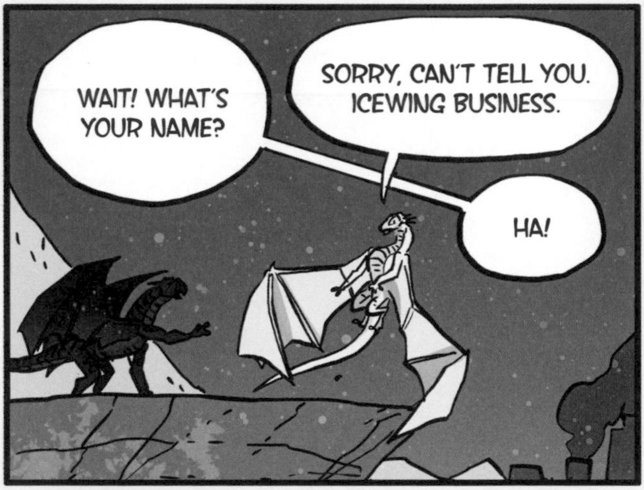

WAIT! WHAT'S YOUR NAME?
SORRY, CAN'T TELL YOU. ICEWING BUSINESS.
HA!

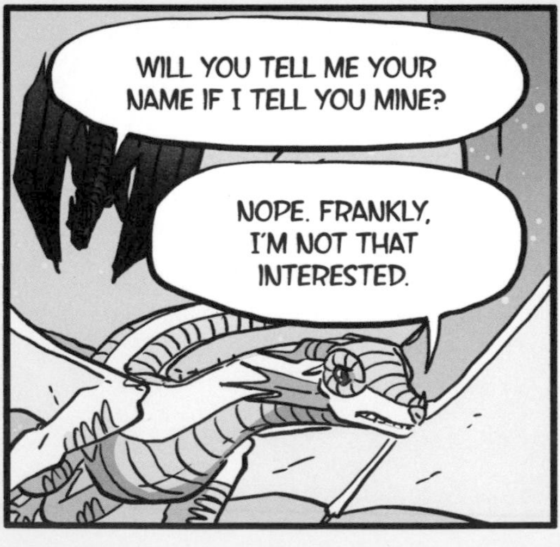

WILL YOU TELL ME YOUR NAME IF I TELL YOU MINE?
NOPE. FRANKLY, I'M NOT THAT INTERESTED.

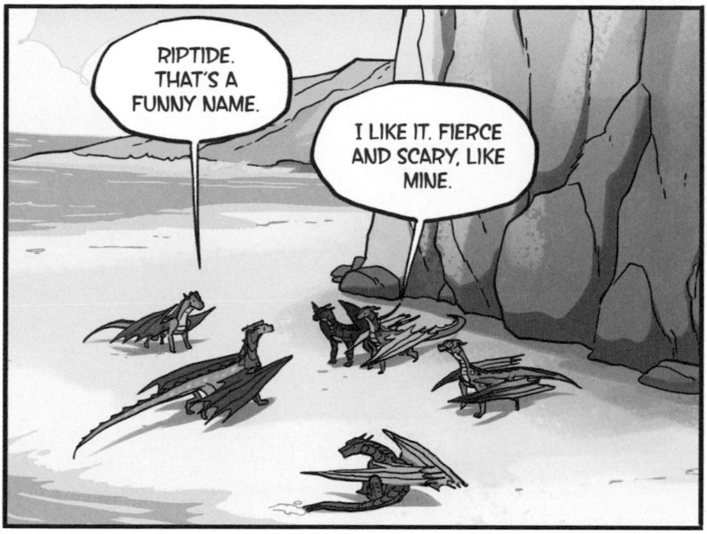
RIPTIDE. THAT'S A FUNNY NAME.
I LIKE IT. FIERCE AND SCARY, LIKE MINE.

Come up with some potential names based on:

Colors:

Plants:

Animals:

Weather:

BOTH CLAY AND TSUNAMI WERE DISAPPOINTED WHEN THEY MET THEIR PARENTS. MAYBE PARENT DRAGONS ARE ALWAYS DISAPPOINTING...
I DON'T EVEN CARE WHAT MY PARENTS ARE LIKE. I JUST WANT TO MEET OTHER RAINWINGS AND SHOW EVERYONE THAT WE'RE MORE THAN LAZY FRUIT EATERS.
RAINWINGS HAVE CAMOUFLAGE SCALES AND SECRET VENOM. I BET WE'RE TOUGHER AND STRONGER THAN ANYONE SUSPECTS!

CREATE YOUR DRAGON

Every adventure needs an interesting character at its center. No matter the conflict, no matter the world, your dragon's choices drive what happens in your story. To understand why they make the choices that they do, you have to understand who your dragon is.

Look back at the dragon you created in Chapter 1, or think about another dragon you love, and write a backstory for them. Where do they come from? Who else is in their family? How does their family treat them? What have they done since the day they hatched? What's the most significant thing that's ever happened to them before the story starts? Where are they now?

TUI TIP

Ask yourself a lot of questions about each character, especially about what made them the way they are.

_____'S

BACKSTORY

DRAW YOUR DRAGON

Creating your own dragon means YOU get to decide exactly what they look like, from the color of their scales, to the shape of their wings, to the length of their tail.

Is your dragon brightly colored like Glory or Kinkajou? Huge like Morrowseer, or tiny like Anemone? Do they have venom-barbed tails like SandWings, or star-speckled wings like NightWings?

On the next page, write your dragon's name in the scroll and create a portrait worthy of hanging on the wall of a queen's palace!

UNDERSTAND YOUR DRAGON

You know your dragon's history, but how well do you really know your dragon's heart?

What powers does your dragon have?

If your dragon could save only one item from a fire, what would it be?

What would your dragon say is most important to them, out of the list below? Pick three to focus on!

family friends hard work loyalty power

learning truth beauty magic adventure honesty

cunning dependability creativity kindness bravery

respect common sense honor adventure patience

justice wit leadership

In your dragon's spare time between adventures, what is their favorite thing to do?

MY CLAWS AREN'T SORE.
I'M NOT ITCHY!
I LOVE IT I LOVE MUD I'M STAYING HERE FOREVER.

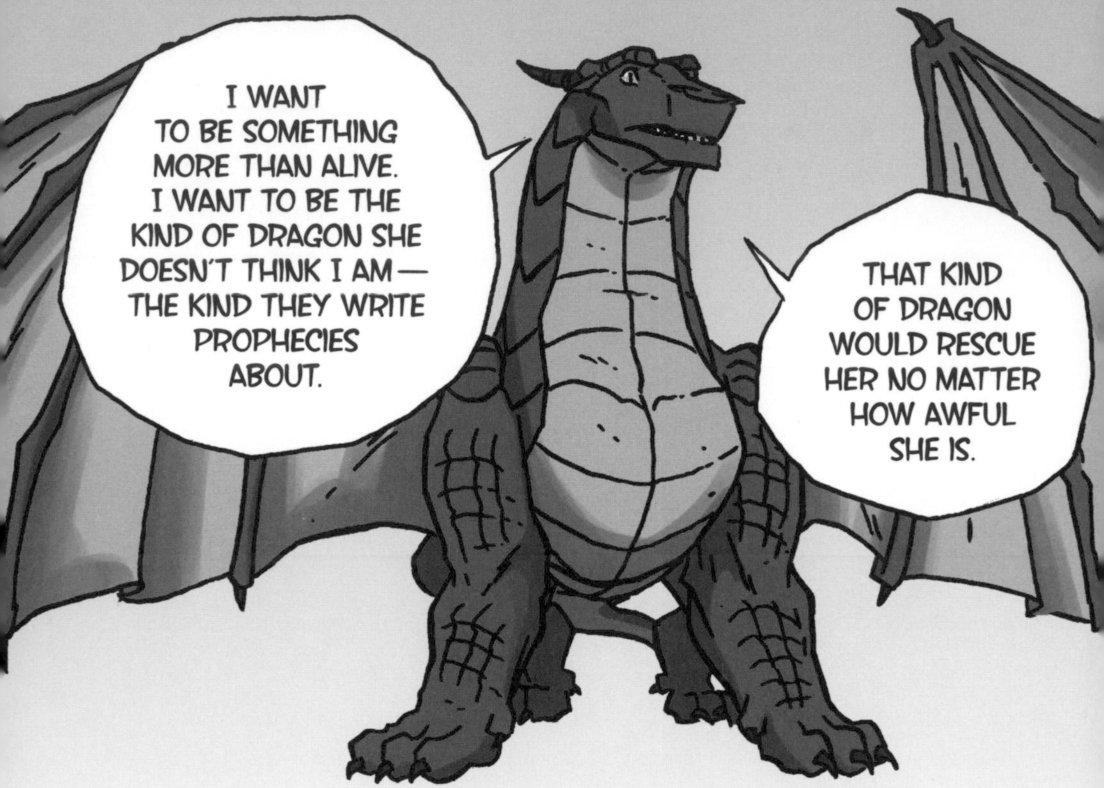
I WANT TO BE SOMETHING MORE THAN ALIVE. I WANT TO BE THE KIND OF DRAGON SHE DOESN'T THINK I AM— THE KIND THEY WRITE PROPHECIES ABOUT.
THAT KIND OF DRAGON WOULD RESCUE HER NO MATTER HOW AWFUL SHE IS.

FIGHT OR FLIGHT?

Dragons are defined not only by what they care about but also how they act. Fill in the blanks with how your dragon would react to these common dragon scenarios.

If your dragon encountered an enemy, they would ______________

____

____

If your dragon found treasure, they would ________________

____

____

If your dragon stumbled upon on a scavenger in the desert, they would

_____

_____

If your dragon was trapped in a cave, they would _____

_____

_____

If your dragon met their parents for the first time, they would

_____

_____

_____

If your dragon found out another dragon had a crush on them,
they would _____

_____

_____

If your dragon was told to read ten scrolls by next week, they
would _____

_____

_____

If your dragon's best friend was captured, they would _____

_____

_____

If your dragon was blown off course while flying, they would

_____

_____

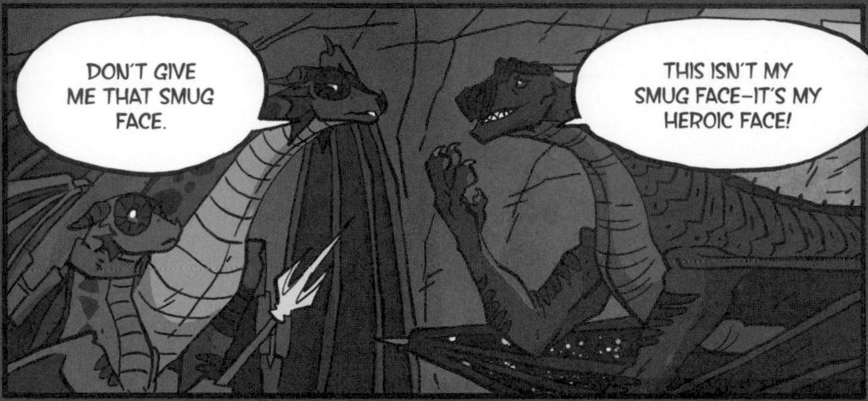
DON'T GIVE ME THAT SMUG FACE.
THIS ISN'T MY SMUG FACE—IT'S MY HEROIC FACE!

EXPRESSIONS AND EMOTIONS

In novels, you can get right inside a character's head. In graphic novels, you can show thoughts in bubbles, but much of what a character feels has to come through in their expressions.

Dragons can be VERY expressive.

Draw your dragon experiencing these emotions:

ANGER • EXCITEMENT • SADNESS
HAPPINESS • HUNGER

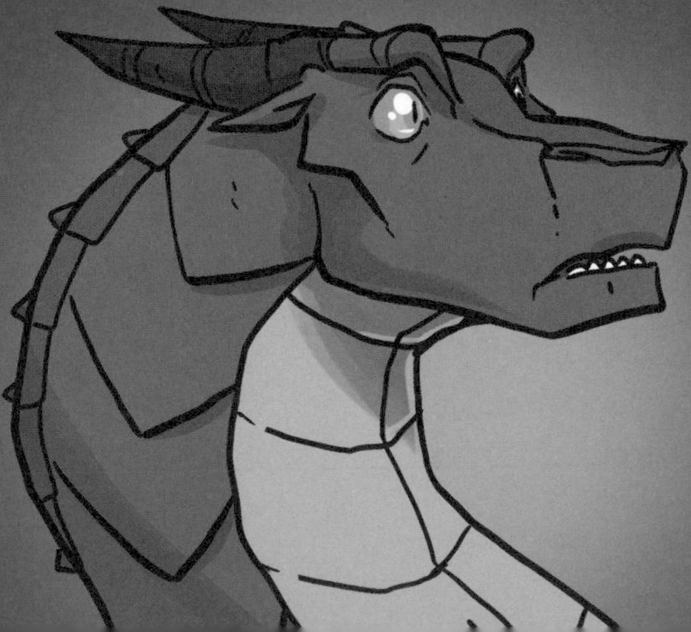

DESCRIBE YOUR DRAGON'S FAMILY

I WONDER WHAT MY PARENTS ARE LIKE.
I WONDER IF ANY OF OUR PARENTS ARE STILL ALIVE.
YOU THINK THEY EVER MISS US?
DEFINITELY. I BET THEY TORE UP THE WORLD LOOKING FOR US.

The dragonets of destiny grew up without their families. They had one another, but it was important to each dragonet to find out more about their parents and siblings and where they came from. Knowing more about your dragon's family will help you understand how they became the dragon they are today.

Create a family tree for your dragon.

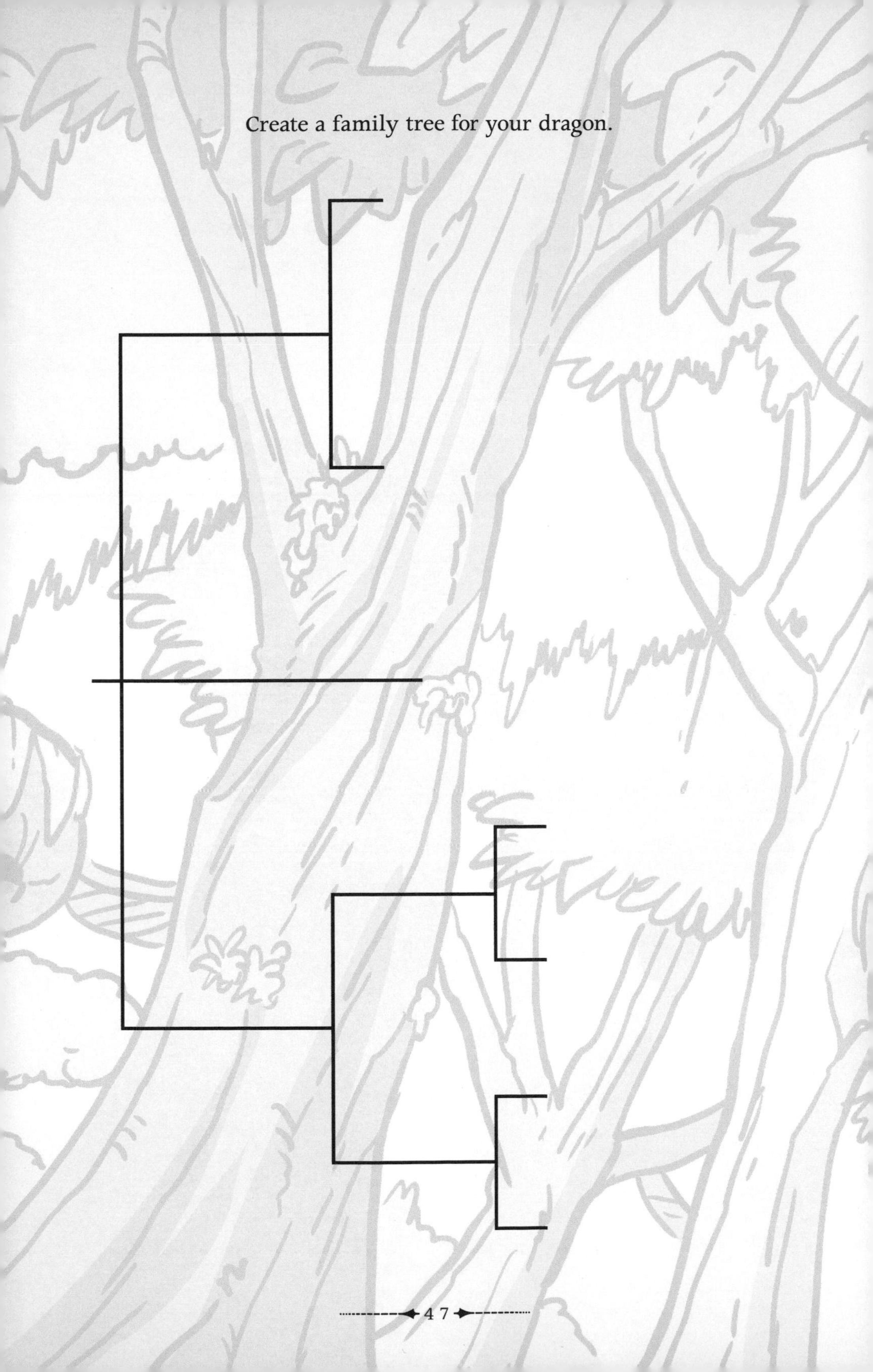

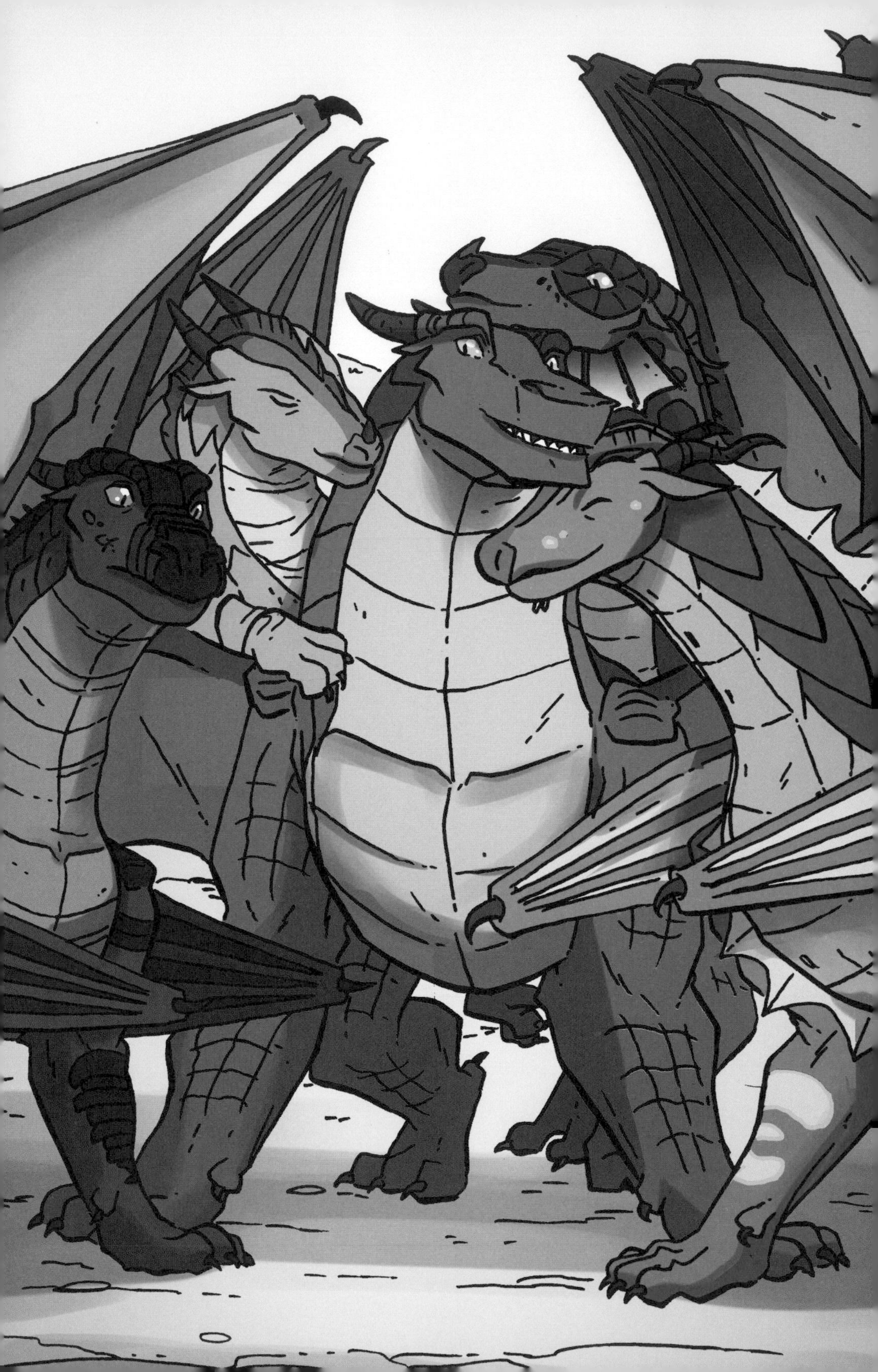

CREATE YOUR DRAGON'S FRIENDS

Your dragon knows their friends at least as well as Clay knows his, and that means you need to get to know them, too! No dragonet can save the world all alone.

On the next few pages, create your dragon's closest friends — and throw in an enemy or two if you get inspired! After all, sometimes enemies can become friends . . .

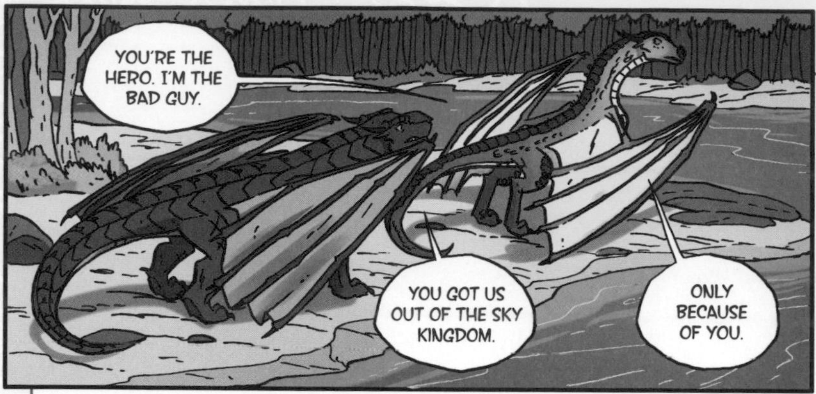
YOU'RE THE HERO. I'M THE BAD GUY.
YOU GOT US OUT OF THE SKY KINGDOM.
ONLY BECAUSE OF YOU.

Name:

Age:

Pronouns:

Tribe:

Size:

Scale coloring:

Powers:

Home:

Family/friends:

Personality:

Name:

Age:

Pronouns:

Tribe:

Size:

Scale coloring:

Powers:

Home:

Family/friends:

Personality:

Name:

Age:

Pronouns:

Tribe:

Size:

Scale coloring:

Powers:

Home:

Family/friends:

Personality:

Name:

Age:

Pronouns:

Tribe:

Size:

Scale coloring:

Powers:

Home:

Family/friends:

Personality:

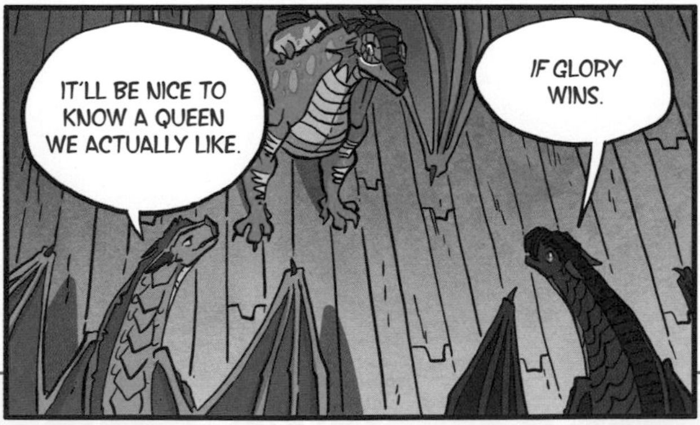
IT'LL BE NICE TO KNOW A QUEEN WE ACTUALLY LIKE.
IF GLORY WINS.

FIND YOUR DRAGON'S VOICE

What your dragon does is important, but what they say and how they say it can also change your story dramatically. Whether you're writing a novel or creating a graphic novel, you have to think about dialogue.

Dialogue can . . .

MOVE THE STORY FORWARD.

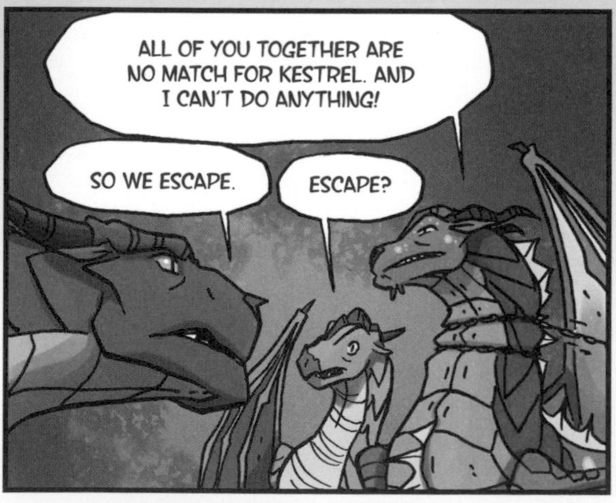
ALL OF YOU TOGETHER ARE NO MATCH FOR KESTREL. AND I CAN'T DO ANYTHING!
SO WE ESCAPE.
ESCAPE?

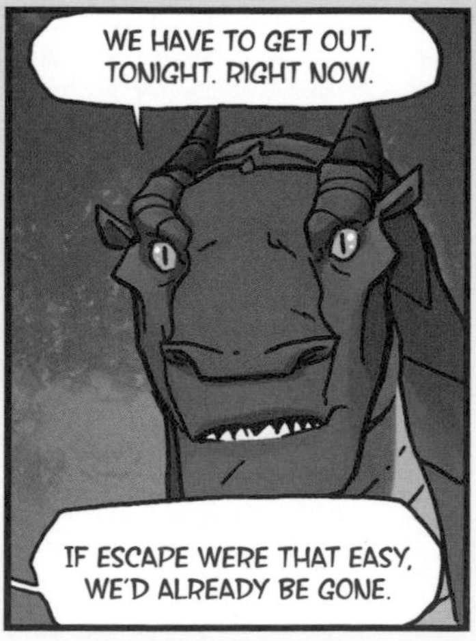
WE HAVE TO GET OUT. TONIGHT. RIGHT NOW.
IF ESCAPE WERE THAT EASY, WE'D ALREADY BE GONE.

PROVIDE A CHARACTER WITH NEW INFORMATION.

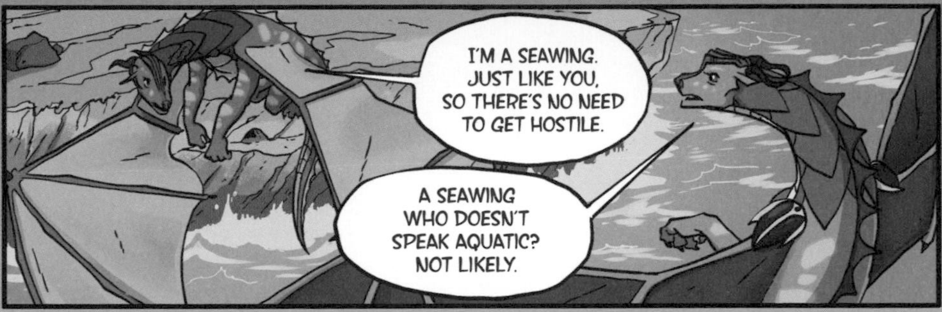
I'M A SEAWING. JUST LIKE YOU, SO THERE'S NO NEED TO GET HOSTILE.
A SEAWING WHO DOESN'T SPEAK AQUATIC? NOT LIKELY.

EXPLAIN HOW THE CHARACTERS FEEL.

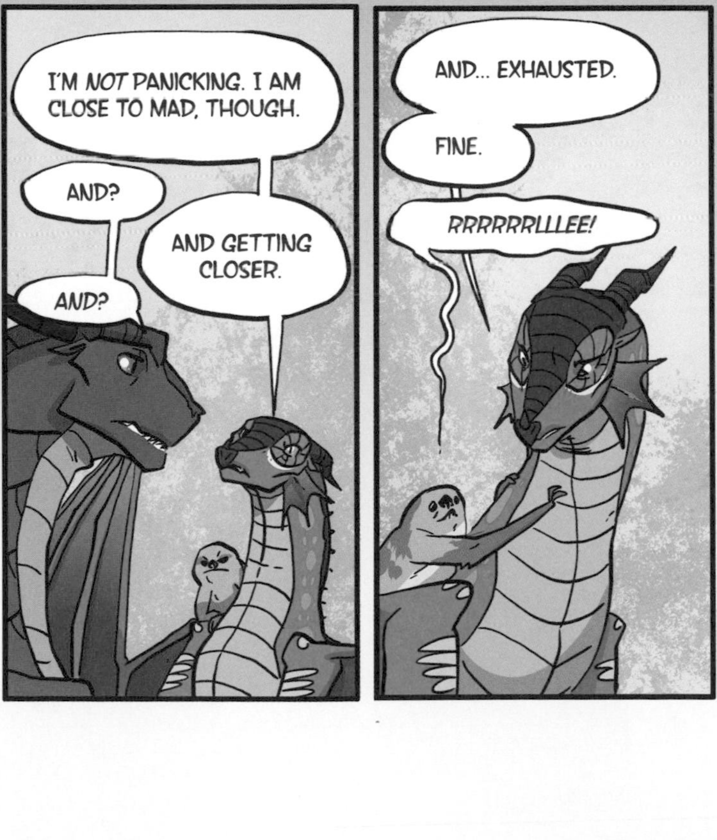
I'M *NOT* PANICKING. I AM CLOSE TO MAD, THOUGH.
AND?
AND GETTING CLOSER.
AND?
AND... EXHAUSTED.
FINE.
RRRRRRLLLEE!

NO TWO DRAGONS SOUND ALIKE . . .

What a dragon says and the words they use to say it tell us so much about their personality. Glory would never say . . .

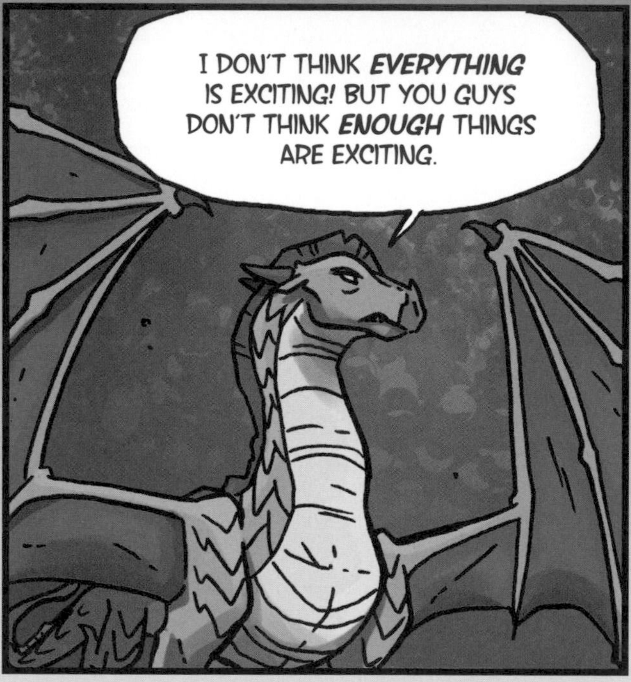
I DON'T THINK *EVERYTHING* IS EXCITING! BUT YOU GUYS DON'T THINK *ENOUGH* THINGS ARE EXCITING.

That's Sunny through and through. But Glory would say . . .

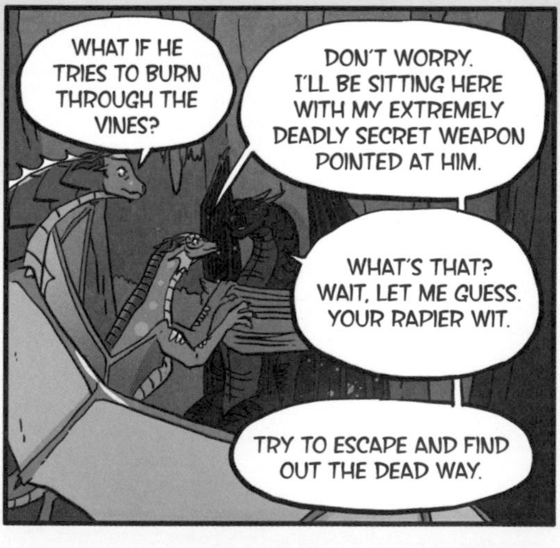
WHAT IF HE TRIES TO BURN THROUGH THE VINES?
DON'T WORRY. I'LL BE SITTING HERE WITH MY EXTREMELY DEADLY SECRET WEAPON POINTED AT HIM.
WHAT'S THAT? WAIT, LET ME GUESS. YOUR RAPIER WIT.
TRY TO ESCAPE AND FIND OUT THE DEAD WAY.

Pick two of your dragons who are totally different from each other and show their completely different responses to receiving VERY bad news.

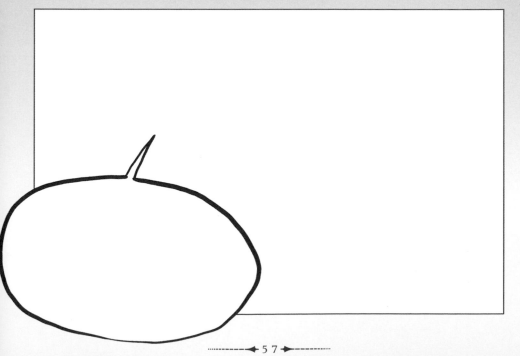

DIALOGUE IN ACTION

Dialogue, depending on who says it and what's happening at the time, can drastically alter the feel of a scene. Think of how Glory and Deathbringer banter even when they're fighting, or how different Tsunami's Aquatic lesson with Whirlpool is from the one she has with Riptide.

Make these scenes your own! Draw dragons to go with the dialogue on the left and write dialogue for the dragons on the right.

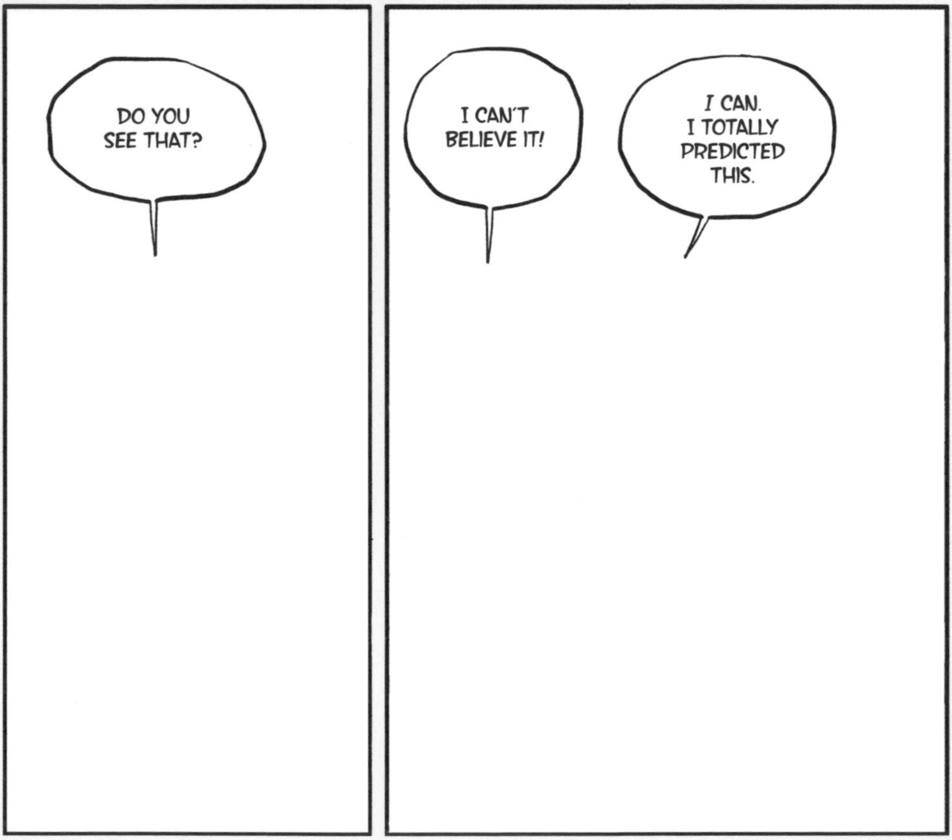
DO YOU SEE THAT?
I CAN'T BELIEVE IT!
I CAN. I TOTALLY PREDICTED THIS.

STORYSTARTER

Write dialogue for a scene where one dragon is trying to extract information from another dragon.

DID YOU FOLLOW US THROUGH THE TUNNEL? OR DID YOU ALREADY KNOW IT WAS THERE?
HOW WOULD *I* KNOW IT WAS THERE?
LET'S TAKE HIM BACK TO THE VILLAGE AND INTERROGATE HIM.
I DON'T THINK THAT'S SAFE FOR THE RAINWINGS.

GLORY, YOU NEVER TOLD US YOU COULD SHOOT VENOM!
I NEVER COULD BEFORE.
BUT *HOW* DID YOU DO IT?
OH, WELL, THERE'S A LOGICAL SCIENTIFIC EXPLANATION AND, *SERIOUSLY, RIGHT* **NOW** *YOU WANT TO HAVE THIS CONVERSATION?*

STORYSTARTER

Write a conversation between dragons who are somewhere they aren't supposed to be.

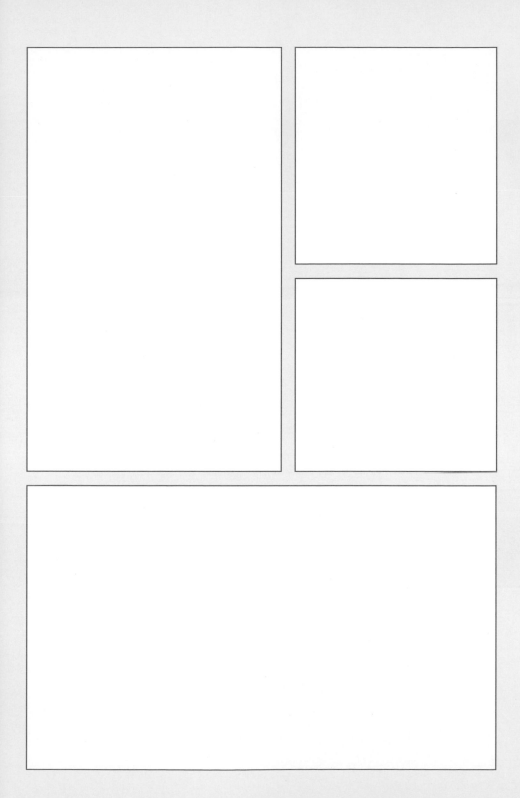

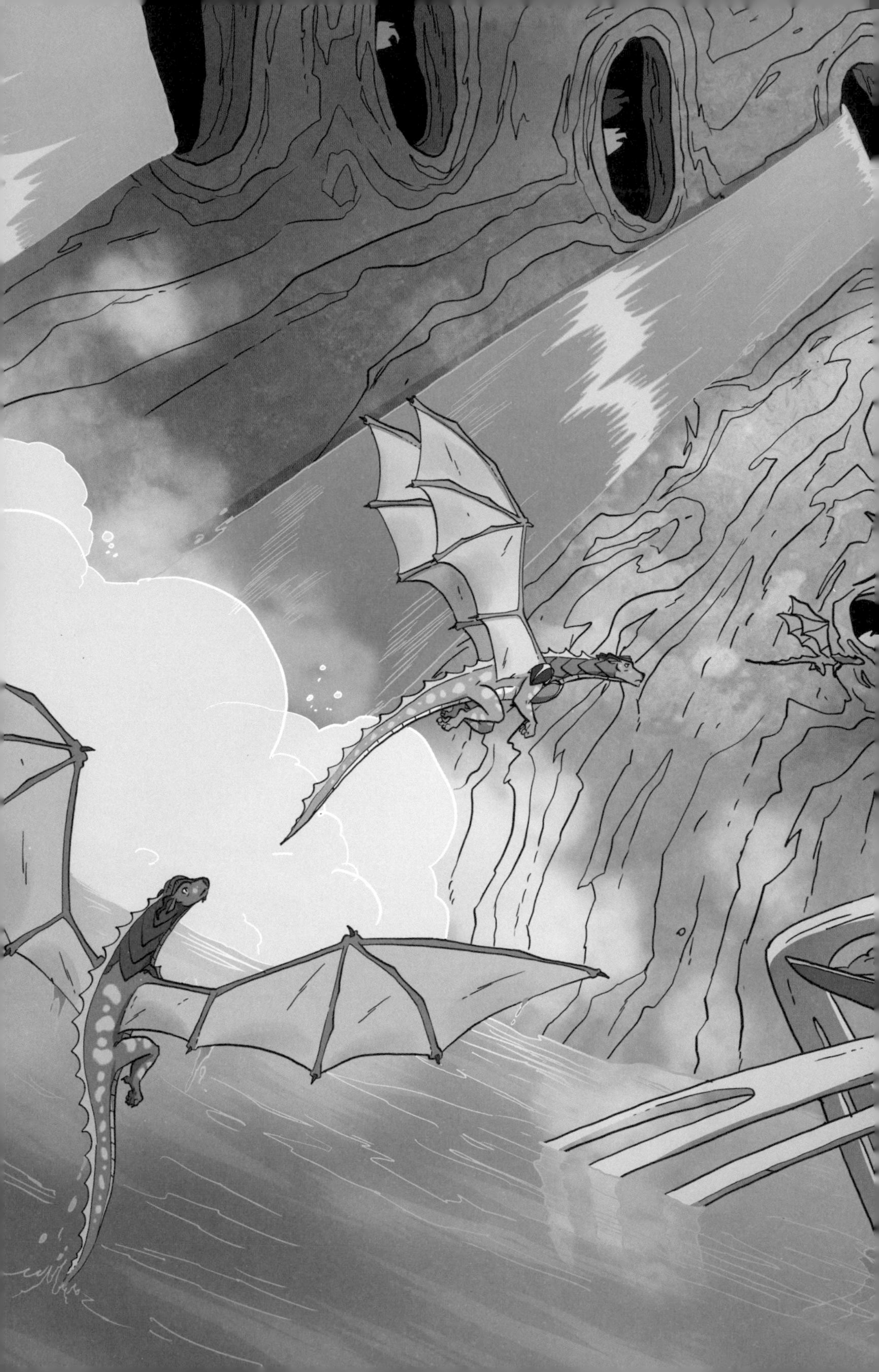

CHAPTER 3

WORLDBUILDING

HISTORY
OF COURSE! WE HAD *LOTS* OF BATTLE TRAINING.
WEBS TAUGHT US THE HISTORY OF PYRRHIA.
HE DID GEOGRAPHY, TOO.
AND DUNE TAUGHT US HUNTING.
KESTREL WAS *SUPPOSED* TO TEACH US ABOUT THE TRIBES, BUT MOSTLY SHE *YELLED* AND TRIED TO *SET* US ON *FIRE*—

DESIGN YOUR CONTINENT

When the dragons you create go on an adventure, their quest may take them across a sprawling, complicated world. Pyrrhia is a huge continent populated by seven different tribes that inhabit vastly diverse environments.

You may start with an idea for what your world looks like and how it works, or you may prefer to discover it with your dragons, one wingbeat at a time. However you build your world, there's one thing you WILL need if you create a fantasy series like Wings of Fire: a map!

Sketch the outlines of your dragon's world! Include important landmarks like palaces, forests, mountains, and deserts. Add to your map as you learn more about the world. You might even find a lost continent as your world expands . . .

TUI TIP

Think of cool places you've been or would like to go . . . Can you include a version of them in your world's map?

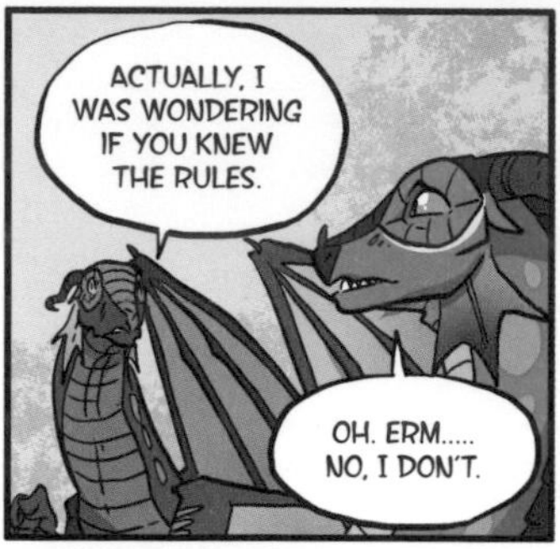
ACTUALLY, I WAS WONDERING IF YOU KNEW THE RULES.
OH. ERM..... NO, I DON'T.

CHOOSE YOUR RULES

Pyrrhia exists in its own universe, but some fantasy stories take place in our world, or in a world with secret portals between one world and another. When creating YOUR dragon world, it's important to know what rules govern it. This means thinking about everything from whether your dragons are at the top of the food chain, like they are in Pyrrhia, to whether magic is part of this world.

Where do your dragons live? Are they in hiding in the remote places on Earth, one of many mystical creatures humans wonder about but rarely see? Do they have their own world, free from any scavenger influence? Or will stepping through a door in your attic that you've never seen before let you sneak into their story?

Create the rules of your world!

SEARCH FOR MAGIC

In Pyrrhia, only animus dragons can cast spells — and they have to have an object to enchant. Too many enchantments and an animus dragon risks turning evil. NightWings can read minds and predict the future — but what if you don't like the future you see or the thoughts that you hear? Magic comes with consequences!

Dragon worlds don't have to be magical. You could create a world where dragons can fly and breathe fire, and even have poisonous tails or venom but can't enchant anything. Or maybe your dragons could all learn to do magic, but only some of them *want* to learn.

What kind of magic would you like to write about? Check off the types of magic you'll include in your world!

☐ Prophecy

☐ Invisibility

☐ Mind reading

☐ Enchanted objects

☐ Enchanted places

☐ Spells

☐ Shape-shifting

☐ Time travel

☐ Teleportation

☐ Other: _____

I DON'T KNOW... SUNNY, THE OTHER TRIBES HAVE BEEN DOING THINGS THEIR WAY FOR HUNDREDS OF YEARS.
SO? THINGS CAN CHANGE. *WE* CAN CHANGE. WE'RE DRAGONS, NOT CATERPILLARS. WE CAN DO THINGS DIFFERENTLY IF WE CHOOSE TO.

RECORD YOUR HISTORY

Your dragons may not be caught up in a prophecy and tasked with ending a war, but the history of your world still affects their adventures. Decisions made by other dragons — or scavengers — decades or hundreds or even thousands of years ago have ripple effects into the present. Queen Oasis's death led to the War of SandWing Succession, but dragons and scavengers have a history that stretches clear back to the Scorching!

TUI TIP Ask yourself questions about how the world got to be this way. Who's in charge? How did they get their power? Has it always been the same family or group, or was there ever a war or revolution that changed the balance of power along the way? Think of the world like a character — the more you know about its backstory, the more interesting it'll be!

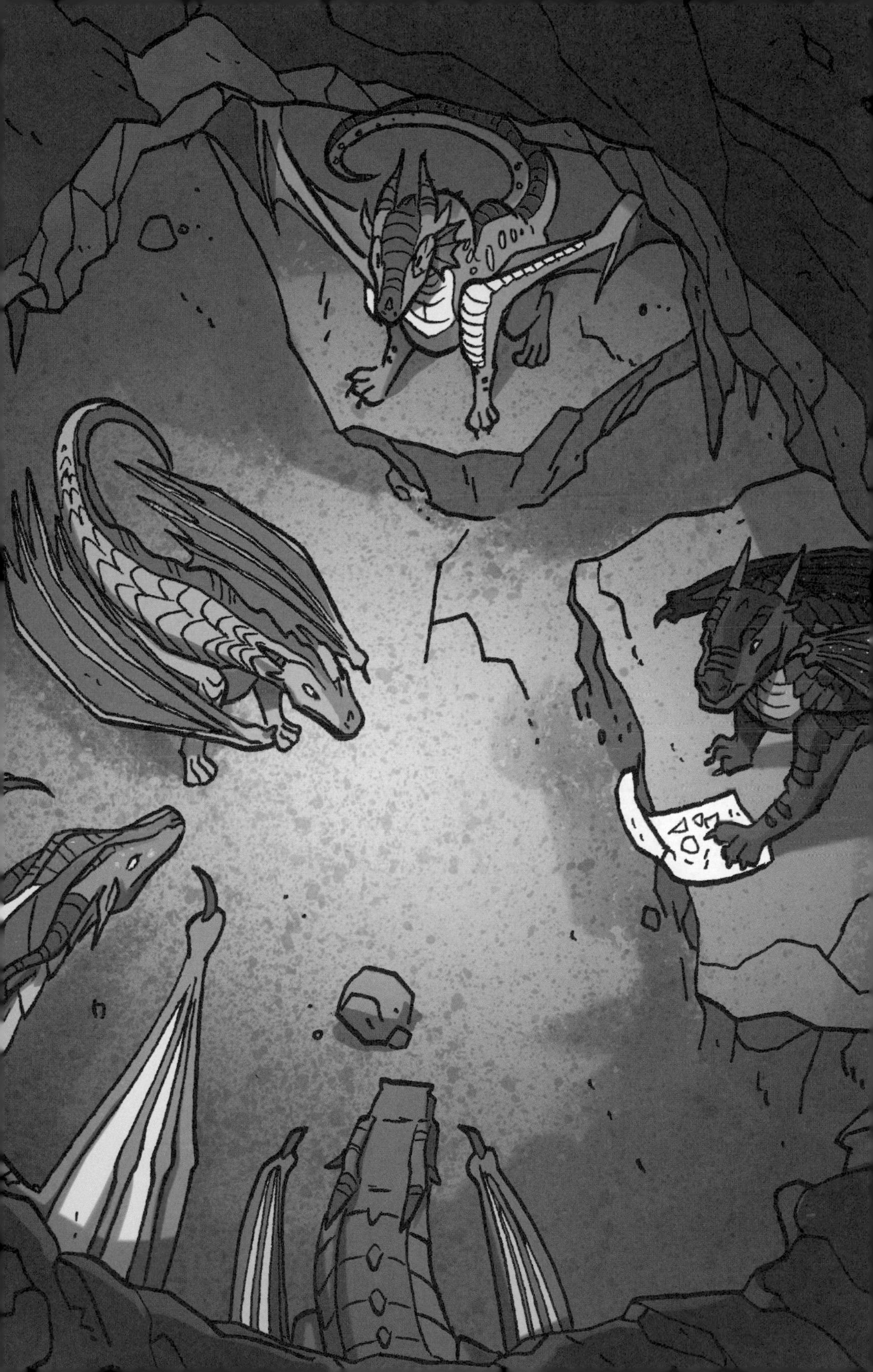

FROM THE SCROLLS OF HISTORY . . .

Create your own scroll describing the epic
events that shaped your world.

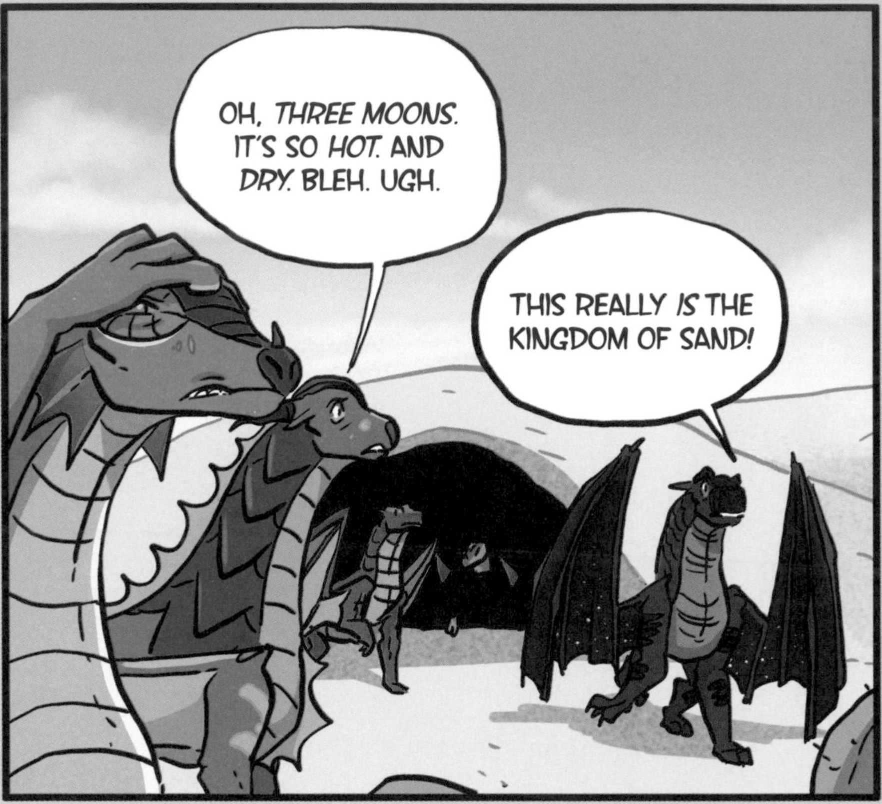
OH, THREE MOONS. IT'S SO HOT. AND DRY. BLEH. UGH.
THIS REALLY IS THE KINGDOM OF SAND!

DESCRIBE YOUR TERRAIN

Pyrrhia is a continent of extremes. The Ice Kingdom and the Kingdom of Sand have totally different climates, and life in the Kingdom of the Sea would be nothing like life in the Rainforest Kingdom. And the NightWing kingdom has its own secret challenges . . .

What does YOUR world look like? Are there dark, mysterious forests? Rolling hills and valleys with cool, clear lakes? Steep mountains with ice caps, or endless canyons of red rock? Do your dragons live on warm islands in the middle of an ocean, or do they build ice palaces next to a glacier?

Describe your world!

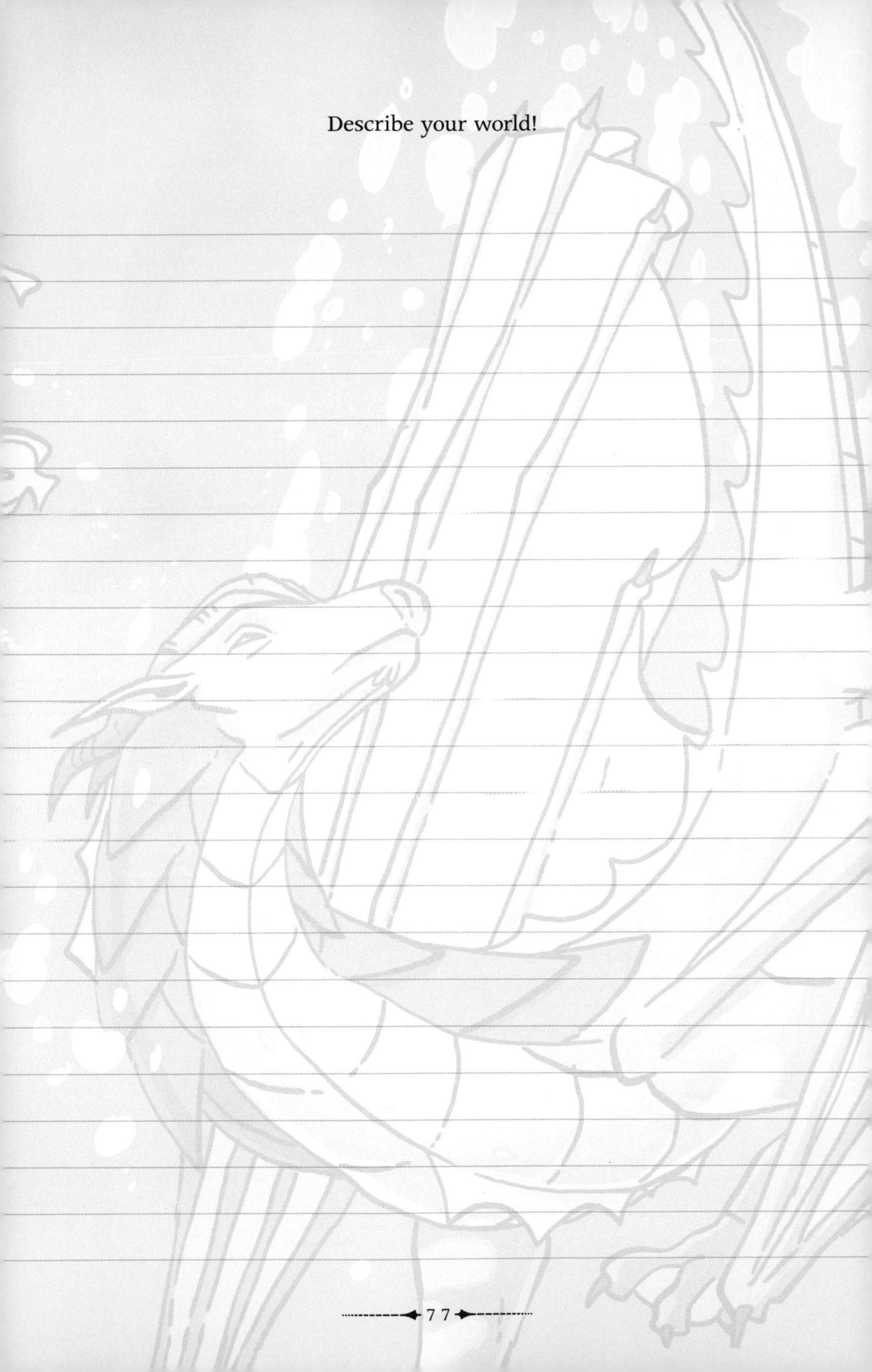

FRIENDLY NEIGHBORS, DEADLY FOES . . .

Pyrrhia may be home to all different tribes of dragons, but other creatures call it home, too. Dragons have learned to coexist with scavengers and sloths, sometimes peacefully and sometimes not so much. And you can find all kinds of different animals across the many habitats of Pyrrhia.

Create the creatures that share your dragon's world!

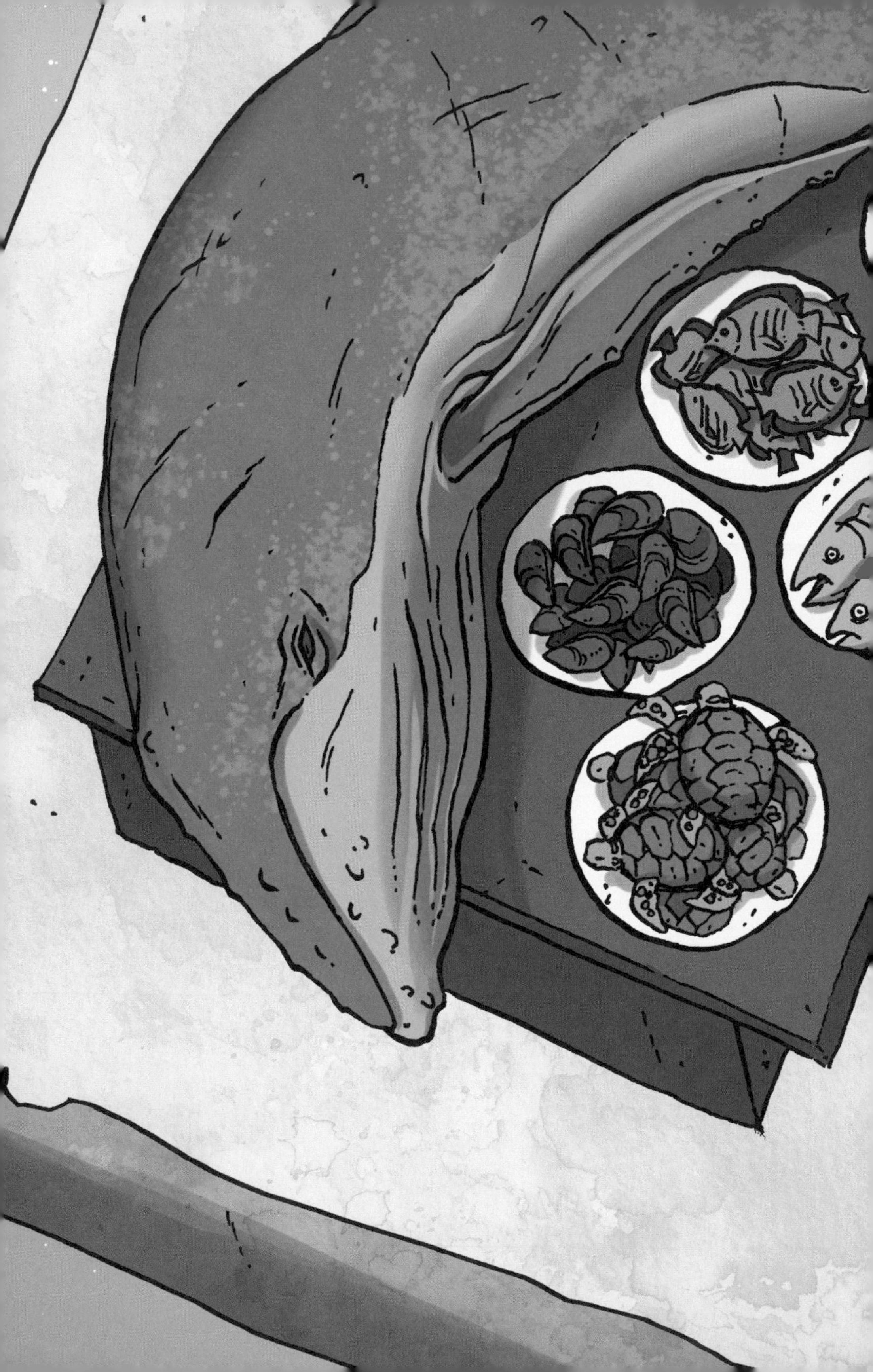

. . . AND TASTY SNACKS

Some of those creatures aren't friends OR foes — they're food! Clay's favorite thing to eat is a cow, but he'd be perfectly happy with a whale . . . or a camel . . . or a polar bear . . . or literally anything edible.

What lives in the world you've created that your dragons might like to eat? Are your dragons carnivores (meat-eaters) or herbivores (vegetarians)? Or happy omnivores who'll eat anything (like Clay!)?

Create a meal your dragons would find delicious!

BUILD YOUR COMMUNITIES

In Pyrrhia, each of the seven tribes has adapted to live well in their kingdom. IceWings can handle the cold of the Ice Kingdom, and RainWings can camouflage their scales to match the lush plant life of the Rainforest Kingdom.

But it's not just their kingdoms that make the tribes distinct. Each tribe has its own unique society. MudWing culture is all about sibling groups. RainWings take turns being queen, or choose their queens through a contest instead of a fight to the death. SeaWings have their own special language, Aquatic. And NightWings prefer to keep secrets from the other tribes.

What makes your dragon communities special? Where do your dragons live? Do your dragons grow up with big families or small ones? How do they pick their leaders?

Create your dragon communities!

MUDWING NESTS ARE REALLY SAFE, SO MOTHERS DON'T CHECK ON THEM OFTEN, YOU KNOW? WE USUALLY HATCH ALONE.
THE FIRST HATCHED IS ALWAYS THE BIGGEST.
THAT'S WHY HE'S THE BIGWINGS!

MUDWINGS HATCHED FROM BLOOD-RED EGGS HAVE FIREPROOF SCALES.
DIDN'T THE TALONS OF PEACE TEACH YOU ANYTHING?

POWERS AND WEAKNESSES

MudWings born from blood-red eggs have fire-resistant scales. RainWings can blend in with their environments. SandWings have their venomous tails, SeaWings can breathe underwater, and several tribes can breathe fire.

Dragons also have their weaknesses, and if they venture too far from home, they might find themselves in trouble.

While fire-breathers don't exist in our world, there ARE reptiles that can spit venom, mammals that can spend a long time under the water, and scorpions with lethal tails.

TUI TIP

Watch nature documentaries and learn about cool animals to get ideas for your dragons!

What special powers and dangerous weaknesses do your dragons have?

POWERS	WEAKNESSES

WILDERNESS AND CIVILIZATION

Dragon homes in Pyrrhia are at least as varied as the different kingdoms. Some dragons live in villages near a river delta, others in palaces of animus-touched ice, and still others in walled cities with narrow, winding streets in the desert.

Do your dragons live in towering skyscrapers or deep in caves underground? Do they hunt in the rainforest for food, or trade for it at a market stall?

Design your dragon's neighborhood.

HOME SWEET HOME

Most dragonets don't grow up under a mountain, but everyone hatches somewhere. Home can be wherever a dragon is with their friends and family. A dragon's home shows us what matters most to them.

Create your dragon's home, from the scrolls on their shelves to the pictures on their walls.

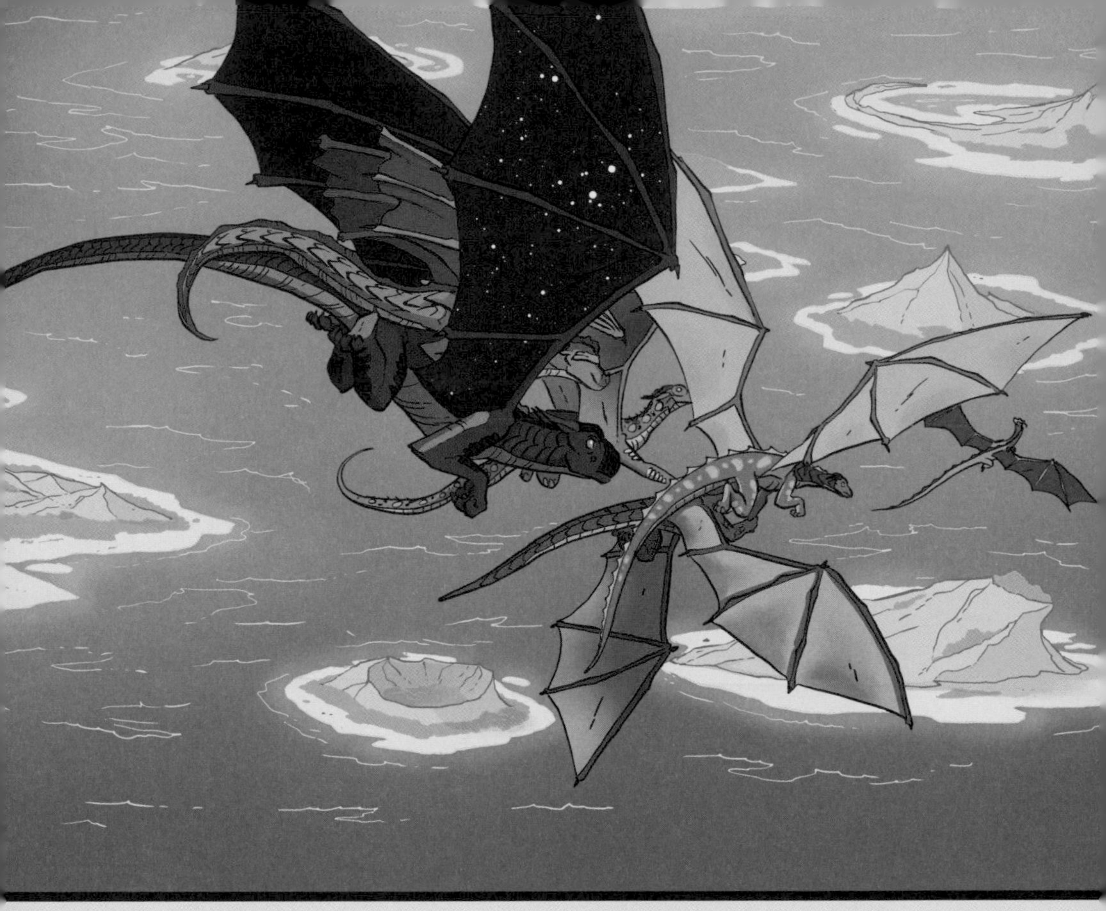

EXPLORE YOUR WORLD

If your dragon explores the world you've created, they may land in environments where they feel totally comfortable and could live forever. Or your dragon might discover a place that's too scary to even visit!

Use these images as starting points to create your world and showcase your dragon's adventures! You can write a story about your dragon's reaction to the environment or draw what they're doing there — or add another dragon and speech bubbles to show us a conversation!

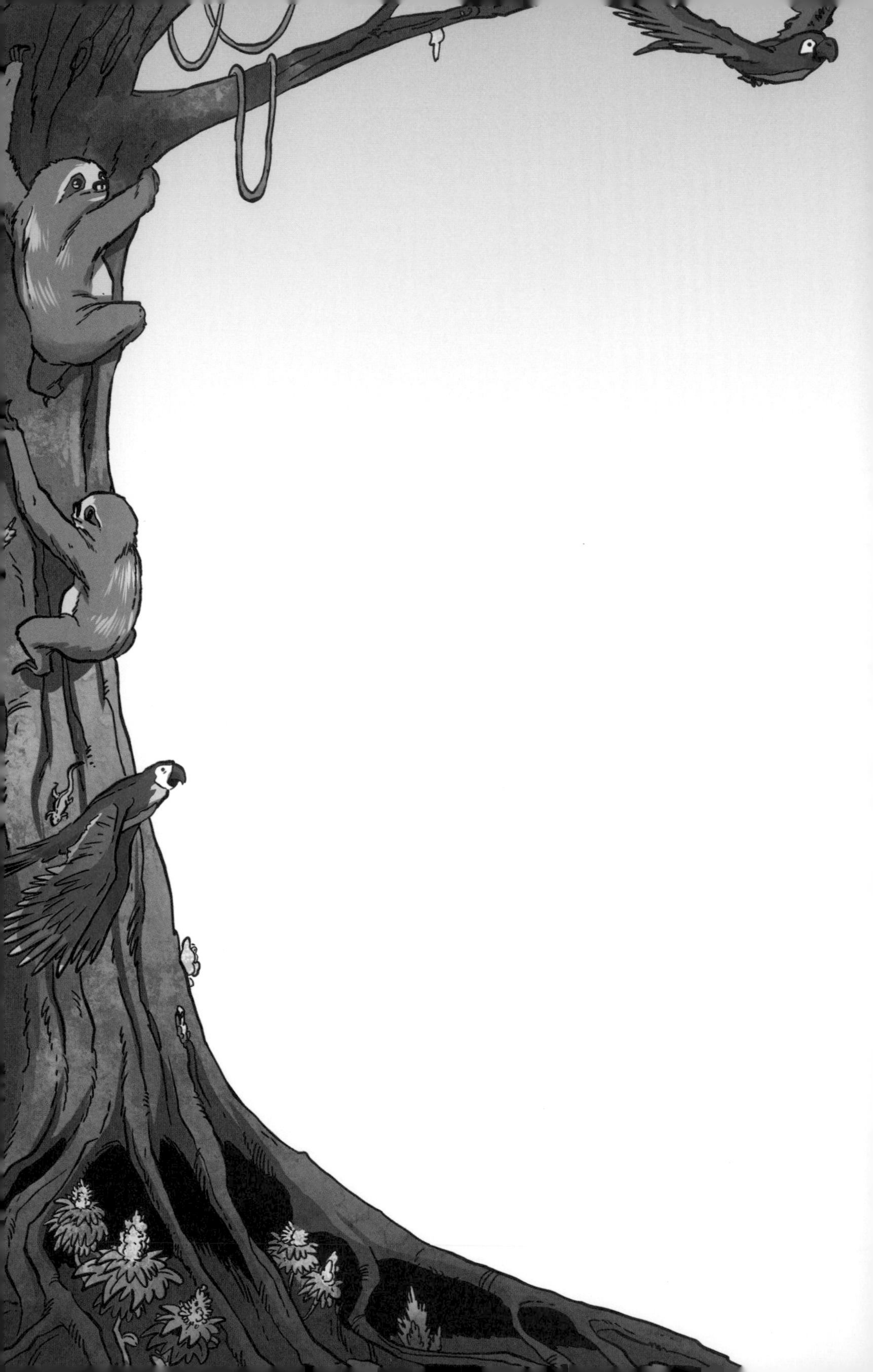

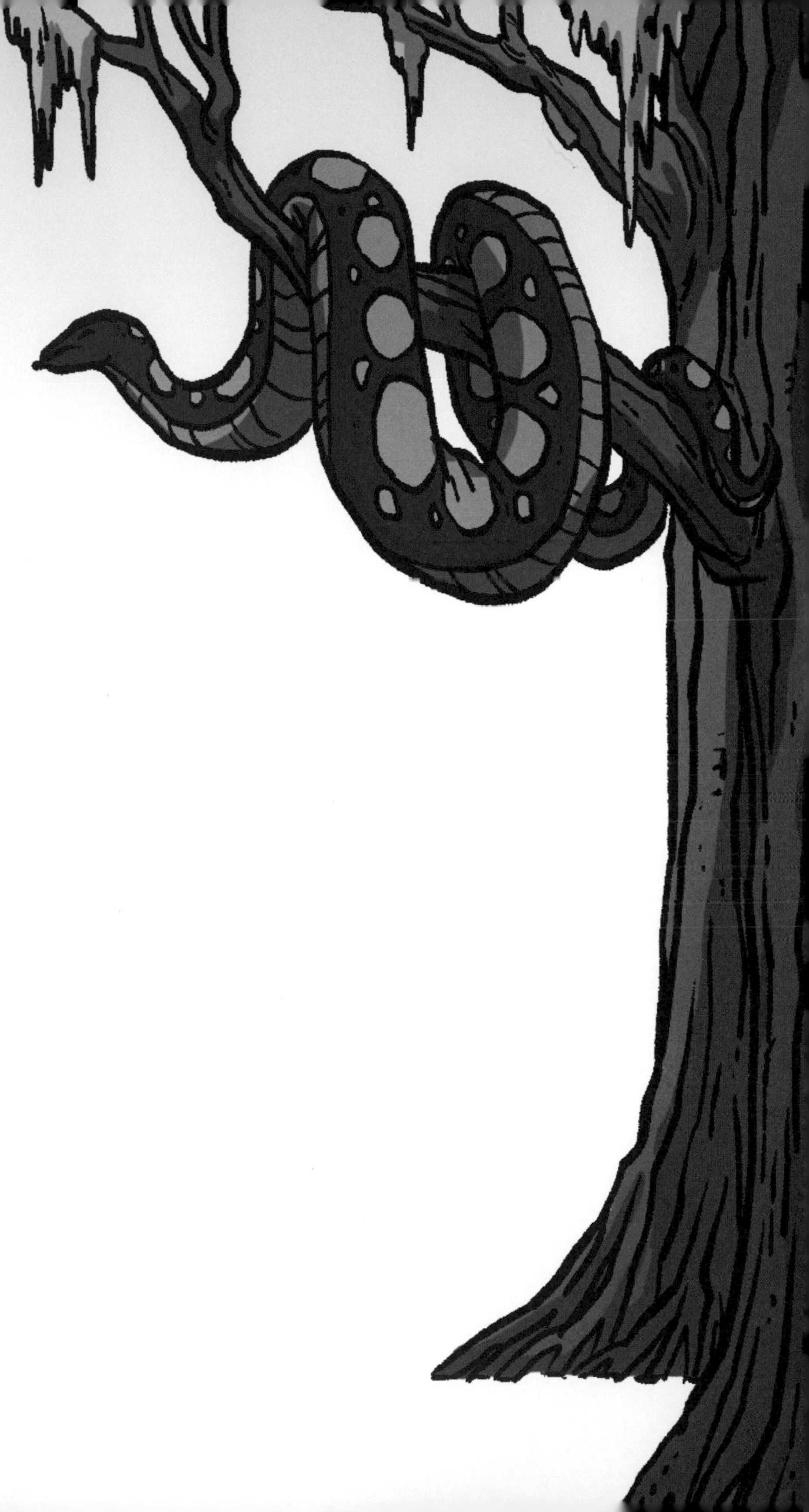

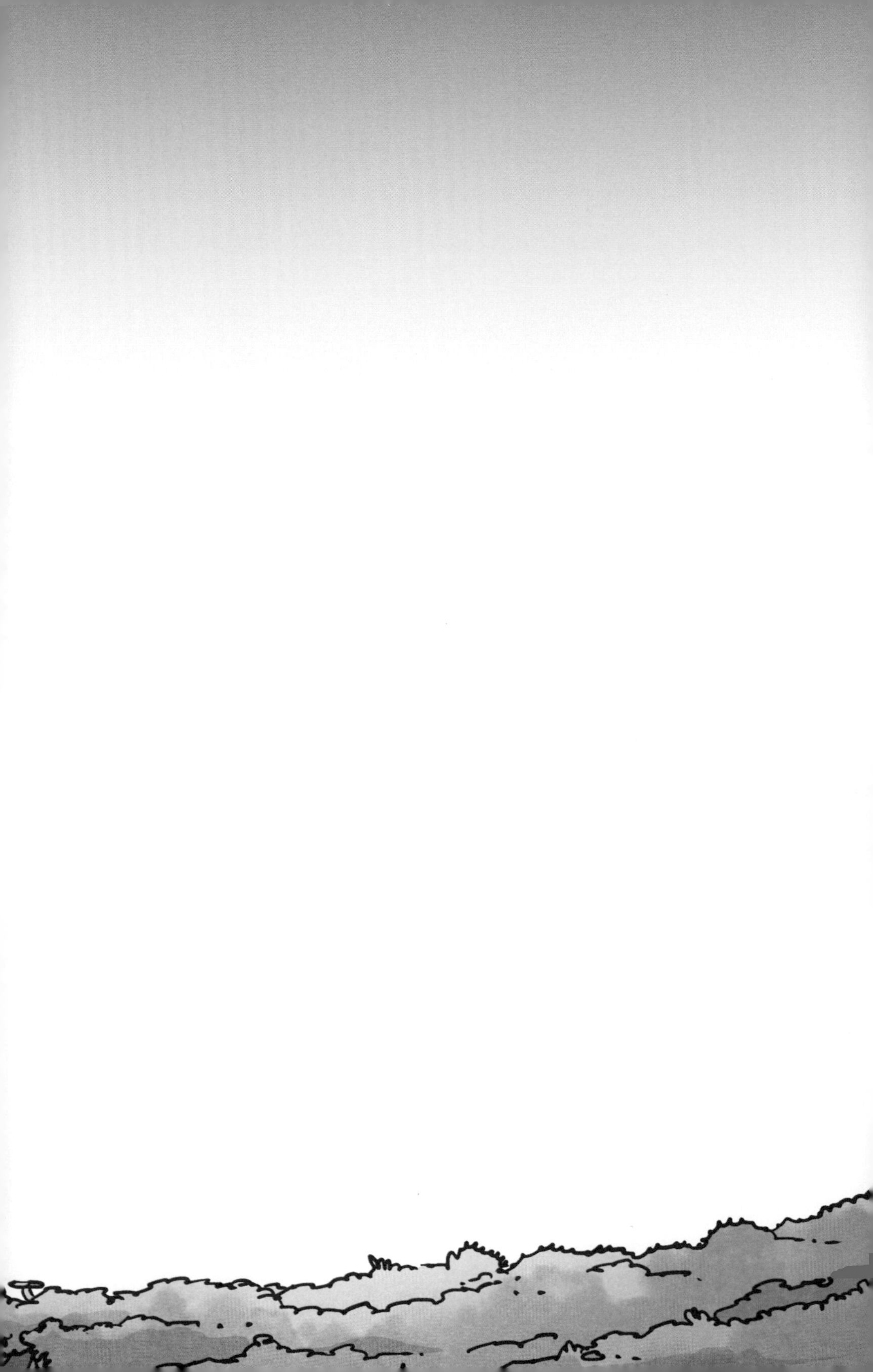

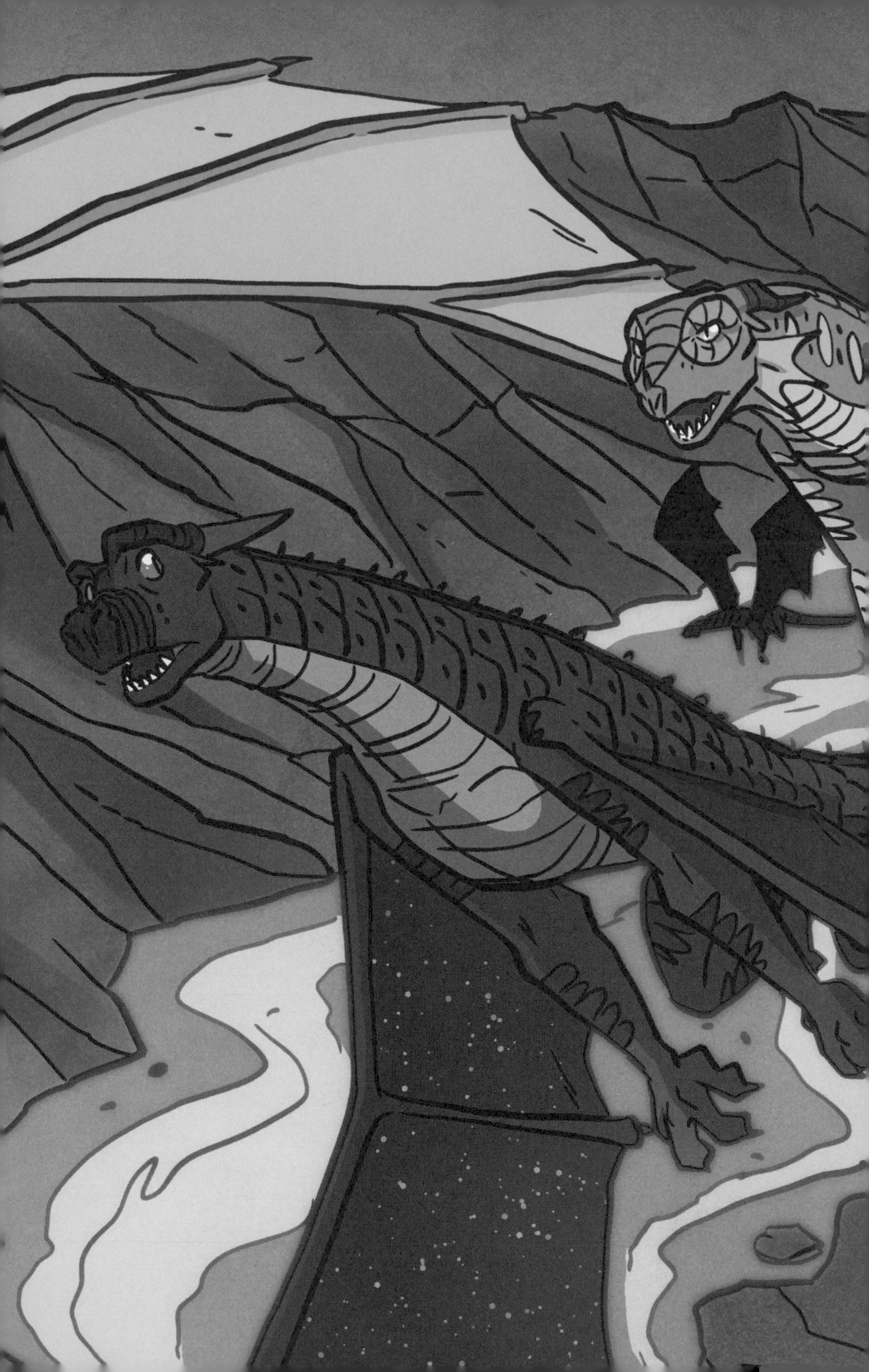

~ CHAPTER 4 ~
FLYING STARTS

CHOOSE YOUR STORY

You've thought about what ideas spark your excitement. You've created dragons you love! And you've built a world you want to explore. You've written dialogue and storystarters, and drawn your characters and your world. It's time to choose your story.

Look back through these pages at what you've created so far. Is there an idea or a character you came back to over and over again? A part of your world that seems as real to you as your own neighborhood? Stories take time and effort to create, so pick an idea that excites you!

I'VE READ THAT ONE! THAT WAS MY FAVORITE STORY EVER!
REALLY? I WROTE IT FOR YOU!
YOU— YOU WROTE THE MISSING PRINCESS?

Write a summary of the story you want to tell! Include the what, who, and where — *what* is happening, *who* your characters are, and *where* the story is taking place. Look at the summaries on the covers of your favorite books to get inspired.

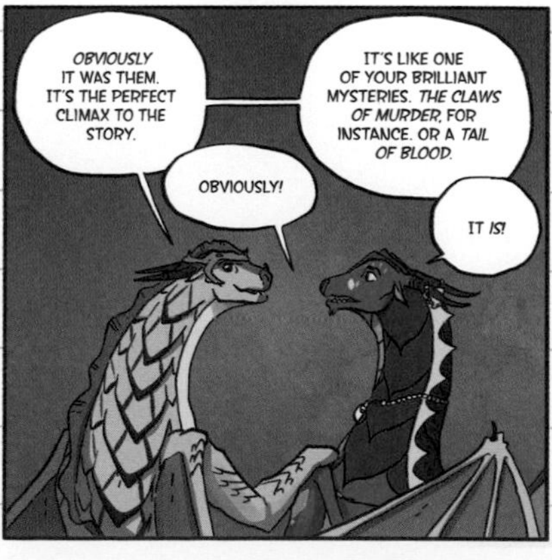
OBVIOUSLY IT WAS THEM. IT'S THE PERFECT CLIMAX TO THE STORY.
IT'S LIKE ONE OF YOUR BRILLIANT MYSTERIES. THE CLAWS OF MURDER, FOR INSTANCE. OR A TAIL OF BLOOD.
OBVIOUSLY!
IT IS!

FIND YOUR FORMAT

Wings of Fire started as a series of novels, and now there are graphic novels, too! When a story is told in one format and then changed so it can be told in another format, it's called an adaptation. Wings of Fire has been adapted into graphic novels; plenty of your other favorite books have been adapted into graphic novels, movies, TV shows, or even for the stage.

Adapting Wings of Fire involves a lot of teamwork! Tui works on the Wings of Fire graphic novels in collaboration with script adapters, the artist, the designer, the letterer, and the colorist. Here's a glimpse of a typical graphic novel process:

Step 1: An author creates a story (like, for instance, a Wings of Fire novel!).

Step 2: That story is crafted into a script. Some scripts are broken down by scene, some by panel. Some are written as dialogue with art direction scattered throughout.

Step 3: The art begins! First, rough sketches are created, either by the author (if they are also an artist) or a dedicated artist. Sketches allow you to see a rough idea of how the panels are working, where certain scenes and lines of dialogue will fall — and give you a chance to change things before more work is done.

Step 4: Once the sketches are all approved, it's time to ink the final art, with dialogue bubbles in place.

Step 5: The final black-and-white art goes off to a colorist to add the colors, and to a letterer to add all the words!

Step 6: The author and editorial team then do a last read to make sure everything looks good, fix any remaining text errors, and then . . . print!

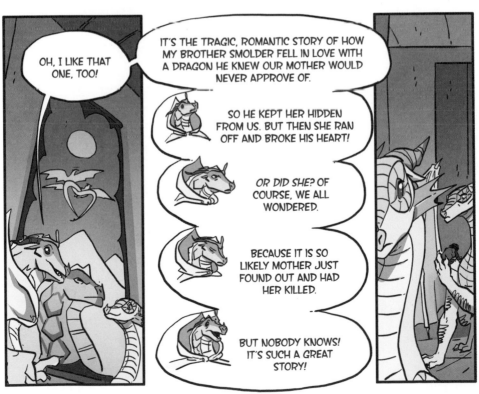

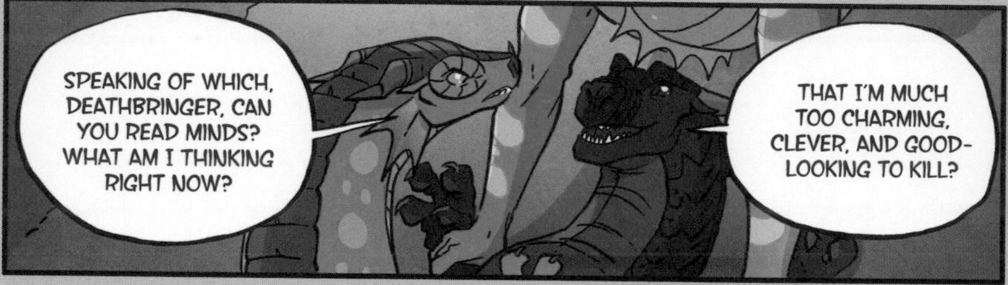
SPEAKING OF WHICH, DEATHBRINGER, CAN YOU READ MINDS? WHAT AM I THINKING RIGHT NOW?
THAT I'M MUCH TOO CHARMING, CLEVER, AND GOOD-LOOKING TO KILL?

NOVELIST OR GRAPHIC NOVELIST?

The world of Pyrrhia is complicated, and the dragons who live there have a lot to say about it. In a novel, you can present a very detailed story, sharing with your reader everything from the deepest history of your world to the innermost thoughts of your characters.

Pyrrhia is a beautiful place with a variety of environments, and the Wings of Fire stories are action-packed with a ton of dialogue. In a graphic novel, you can show readers your vision of your world and your characters, from your dragon's exact expression when they're upset to the grandeur of a royal palace.

What is the right format for YOUR story? If you love writing about your characters' thoughts and describing your world and history, you might prefer to write a novel.

If you love writing fast-paced action and witty dialogue paired with gorgeous art, you might want to try a graphic novel.

In the pages ahead, you will see how one Wings of Fire scene went from novel to script to graphic novel, and you'll have the chance to do the same for your story.

You don't have to be both an artist AND a writer to be a graphic novelist. Collaborating is awesome!

If you know that a graphic novel is the right format for your story, but you don't enjoy drawing, find a friend who does! You can write the story and the script, and your friend can create the art.

Or maybe you LOVE drawing and you have a friend who writes the funniest dialogue. Work together and create a story you love!

Working with a friend on a novel can be fun, too! Take turns writing chapters or trade off writing the dialogue and the description.

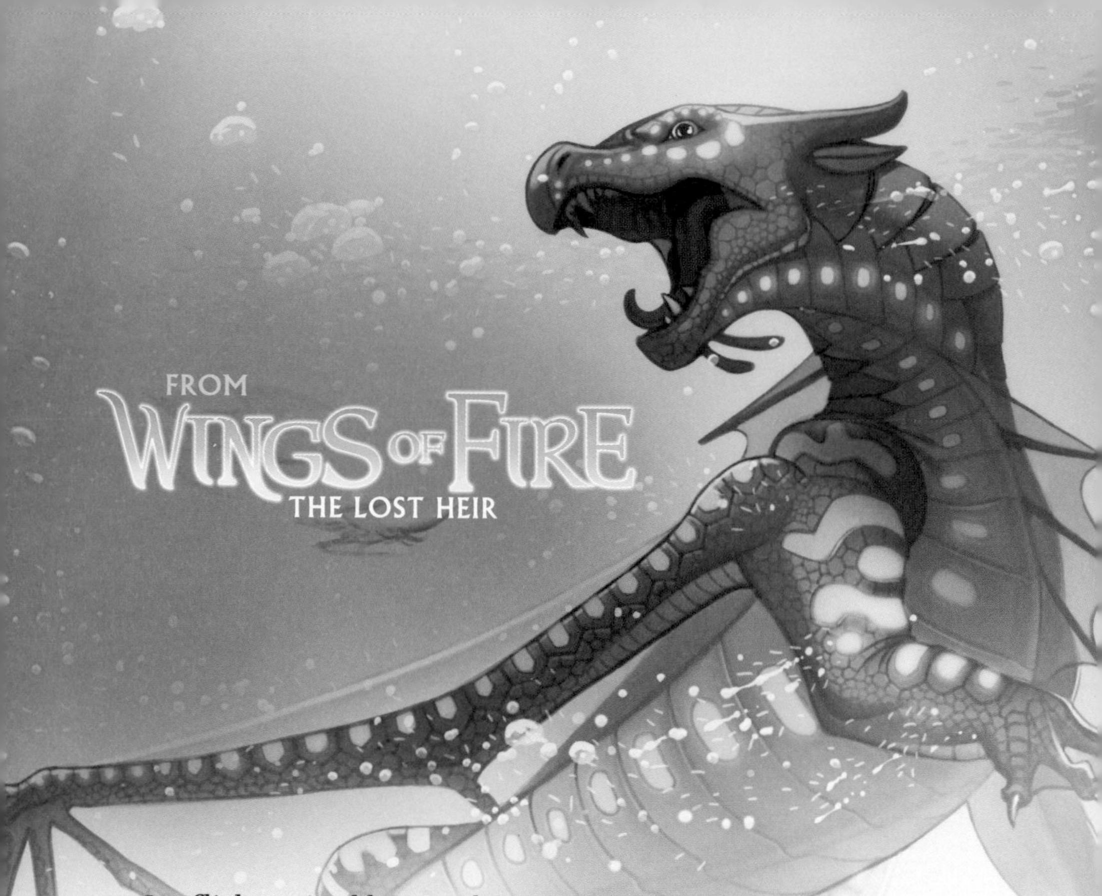
FROM
WINGS OF FIRE
THE LOST HEIR

Starflight arrived last, catching on to the side and pitching forward as if his wings had barely been strong enough to carry him. He lay there like a woeful black puddle for a moment, taking deep breaths. Sunny hopped over a watery footprint to nudge his wing gently.

Tsunami managed not to roll her eyes, but really. Couldn't everyone at least *try* to act a *little* more impressive?

"This is a really big thing!" Clay said to her and Riptide. His tail accidentally splashed Glory, but she was too busy looking at the throne to snap at him. "I mean, this thing we're standing on. What do you call it? It's really tall — taller than our prisons in the Sky Kingdom, I think." He peered over the edge, missing Riptide's sharp look. Tsunami realized they hadn't told him about being captured by Queen Scarlet and the SkyWings.

"I like it," Clay went on, sitting down and splashing Glory again. "Of course, it's much nicer to be this high when your wings are free. But at least the SkyWings gave us a pig sometimes. Do you have pigs? Octopi would be all right instead if you don't. Or squid. Or manatees. I could go for a manatee right now. Or a whale. I'm not fussy, is what I'm saying. Say, how did you make this big thing? Did it take forever to build?"

Riptide blinked for a moment, following Clay's train of thought. "The pavilion? An animus SeaWing designed it, many generations ago, and magicked the stone to grow this way," Riptide said. "Even so, it took nearly ten years to reach this form."

"Wow," said Clay, and Tsunami couldn't help being impressed, too. She hadn't realized animus dragons had that kind of power. In their lessons, Webs had told them animus dragons could enchant chess pieces to play themselves. Sometimes they left curses on their jewels to poison anyone who tried to steal them. But making a whole pavilion grow from stone — that seemed like strong magic, more powerful than anything the NightWings could do.

Starflight was clearly thinking the same thing, judging from his disgruntled snout. Tsunami hurriedly interrupted before he could begin a lecture.

"This top level is where Queen Coral meets new visitors, like us," she said importantly to her friends. "So when she arrives, everyone *please* act like dragonets of destiny instead of half-drowned seagulls, for goodness' sake."

Sunny looked wounded, and Starflight sniffed loudly while Glory turned up her snout like she wasn't taking any orders from Tsunami. Clay poked his nose over the edge and blinked at the lower pavilion tiers.

"Which level is the feasting on?" he asked. "You do have feasting, right?" His wide brown eyes turned to Riptide. "No reason. Just wondering."

"Sure, sometimes we have feasts," Riptide said. "Especially when Queen Blister is —"

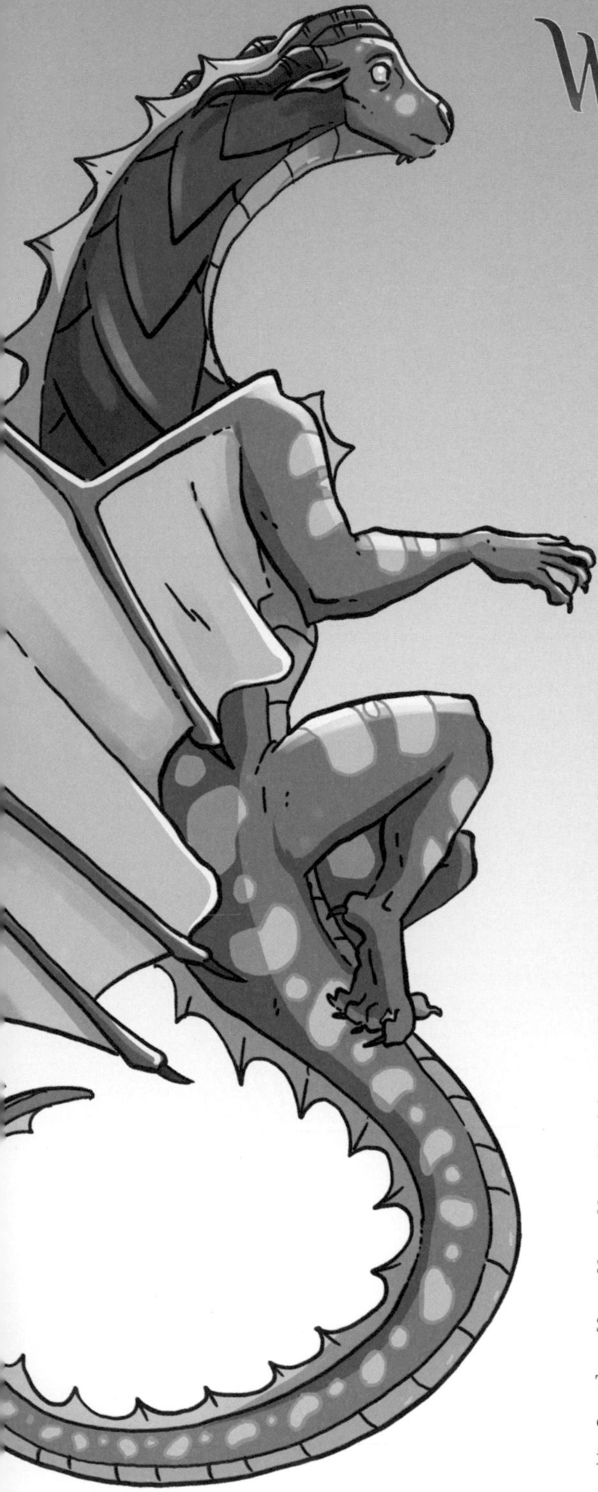

FROM

WINGS OF FIRE

THE LOST HEIR
THE GRAPHIC NOVEL

CLAY: This is a really big thing! I mean, this thing we're standing on. It's really tall — even taller than our prisons in the Sky Kingdom, I think.

CLAY: Of course, it's much nicer to be this high when your wings are free. But at least the SkyWings gave us a pig sometimes. Do you have pigs? Say, how did you make this thing? Did it take forever to build?

RIPTIDE: The pavilion? An animus magicked the stone many centuries ago.

CLAY: Wow.

TSUNAMI: I didn't know an animus could do that.

CLAY: What level is the feasting on? I could really go for a whale right now. Or an octopus. Or some squid. What I'm saying is, I'm not fussy. You *do* have feasting, right?

RIPTIDE: Sure, sometimes we have feasts. Especially when Queen Blister is —

STARFLIGHT: GASP. PANT.

STARFLIGHT: GASP! GASP!

STARFLIGHT: PAAAAAAAANT.

TSUNAMI: When Queen Coral arrives, could everyone please *try* to be more impressive?

THIS IS A REALLY BIG THING! I MEAN, THIS THING WE'RE STANDING ON. IT'S REALLY TALL—EVEN TALLER THAN OUR PRISONS IN THE SKY KINGDOM, I THINK.

OF COURSE, IT'S MUCH NICER TO BE THIS HIGH WHEN YOUR WINGS ARE FREE. BUT AT LEAST THE SKYWINGS GAVE US A PIG SOMETIMES. DO YOU HAVE PIGS? SAY, HOW DID YOU MAKE THIS THING? DID IT TAKE FOREVER TO BUILD?

THE PAVILION? AN ANIMUS MAGICKED THE STONE MANY CENTURIES AGO.

WOW.

I DIDN'T KNOW AN ANIMUS COULD DO THAT.

WHAT LEVEL IS THE FEASTING ON? I COULD REALLY GO FOR A WHALE RIGHT NOW. OR AN OCTOPUS. OR SOME SQUID. WHAT I'M SAYING IS, I'M NOT FUSSY. YOU DO HAVE FEASTING, RIGHT?

SURE, SOMETIMES WE HAVE FEASTS. ESPECIALLY WHEN QUEEN BLISTER IS—

GASP. PANT.

GASP! GASP!

PAAAAAAAANT.

WHEN QUEEN CORAL ARRIVES, COULD EVERYONE PLEASE TRY TO BE MORE IMPRESSIVE?

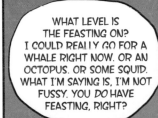

Decide whether your story should be a novel or a graphic novel by creating the same scene in both formats. On this spread, write a scene from your story. Include conflict, dialogue, and descriptions of your world.

Turn your scene into a graphic novel script! Label dialogue with characters' names and include notes for art.

Turn your script into a comic! Add images and speech bubbles to these panels.

> IF NIGHTWINGS CAN ACTUALLY SEE THE FUTURE, WHY BE ALL CRYPTIC AND VAGUE? WHY NOT GIVE US A *USEFUL* PROPHECY LIKE, "BY THE WAY, BLAZE IS GOING TO WIN, SO DON'T EVEN BOTHER FIGHTING."

PLAN YOUR PATH

When you're ready to sit down and start creating, sometimes it can help to look ahead and think about where you want your story to go. This can be as simple as having a vague idea of what happens next or as detailed as creating a chapter-by-chapter outline of what will happen when.

Whether you decide to outline your story or not, be open to surprise twists and turns along the way! You never know when a certain minor IceWing character or a throwaway line about a scary NightWing legend might become much more important than you expected.

TUI TIP Outlining isn't for everyone! It's okay if you like to jump right in and see where the story takes you. I like to spend a lot of time on backstory and characters and then discover the plot as I go — but I always have a few of the big story twists planned ahead of time!

Want to try outlining? Write about your story path here!

Beginning:

Middle:

End:

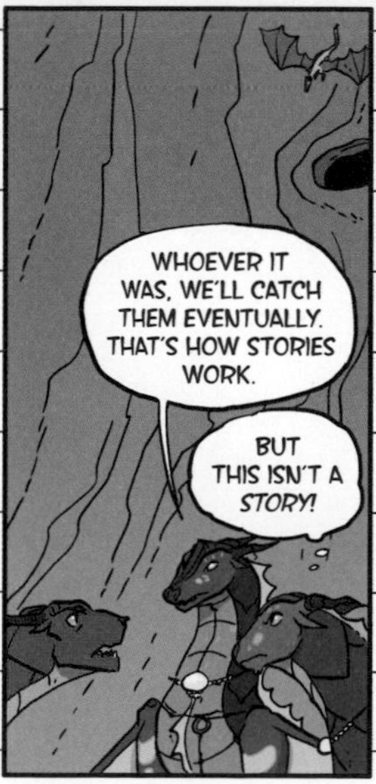
WHOEVER IT WAS, WE'LL CATCH THEM EVENTUALLY. THAT'S HOW STORIES WORK.
BUT THIS ISN'T A *STORY*!

TITLE YOUR WORK

In Chapter 1, we talked about how some creators like to start with a conflict, others with a character, and others with a place. Each of these ideas becomes the story's core, and a good title hints at the heart of a story, just like these Wings of Fire titles . . .

CONFLICT

The Dragonet Prophecy: dragonets with a destiny

The Lost Heir: the return of a missing princess

CHARACTERS

Winter Turning: a frosty IceWing loses his chill — just a little

Escaping Peril: a dangerous SkyWing loses herself to find out who she is

PLACE

The Hidden Kingdom: *two* kingdoms with secrets

The Lost Continent: a whole new dragon world to explore

I KNOW WHERE WE ARE.

THIS IS THE SECRET HOME OF THE NIGHTWINGS.

There are three main structures for Wings of Fire titles (so far!). These structures are built from these basic parts of speech:

• Nouns: a person, place, or thing (such as *prophecy* or *heir*).

• Proper Nouns: the name of a person, place, or thing (such as *Clay*, *Glory*, or *Peril*).

• Adjectives: a word that describes a noun (such as *lost* or *dark*).

• Verbs: a word that describes an action or state of being (such as *turn* or *escape*).

• Gerunds: a special kind of noun created by adding *-ing* to a *verb* (such as *turning* or *escaping*).

Create your own titles!

The [Adjective] [Noun] (*The Lost Heir*)

The _____ _____

The _____ _____

The _____ _____

[Proper Noun] [Gerund] (*Moon Rising*)

_____ _____

_____ _____

_____ _____

[Noun] of [Noun] (*Talons of Power*)

_____ of _____

_____ of _____

_____ of _____

MAKE A COVER

A great cover compels readers to discover the story inside a book's pages. Every Wings of Fire book has a gorgeous cover that invites readers into the world. These covers follow a few design guidelines that might help YOU create your own beautiful dragon cover.

Let's look at the cover for *The Dangerous Gift*!

1. This cover has one large central image of a dragon in action!

2. This cover is in vibrant color, with strong contrast between the dragon and the background.

3. All the words on this cover, from the series title to the book title and the author's credit, are easy to read.

4. This cover has a detailed background that provides context about the book's setting but doesn't distract from the main character.

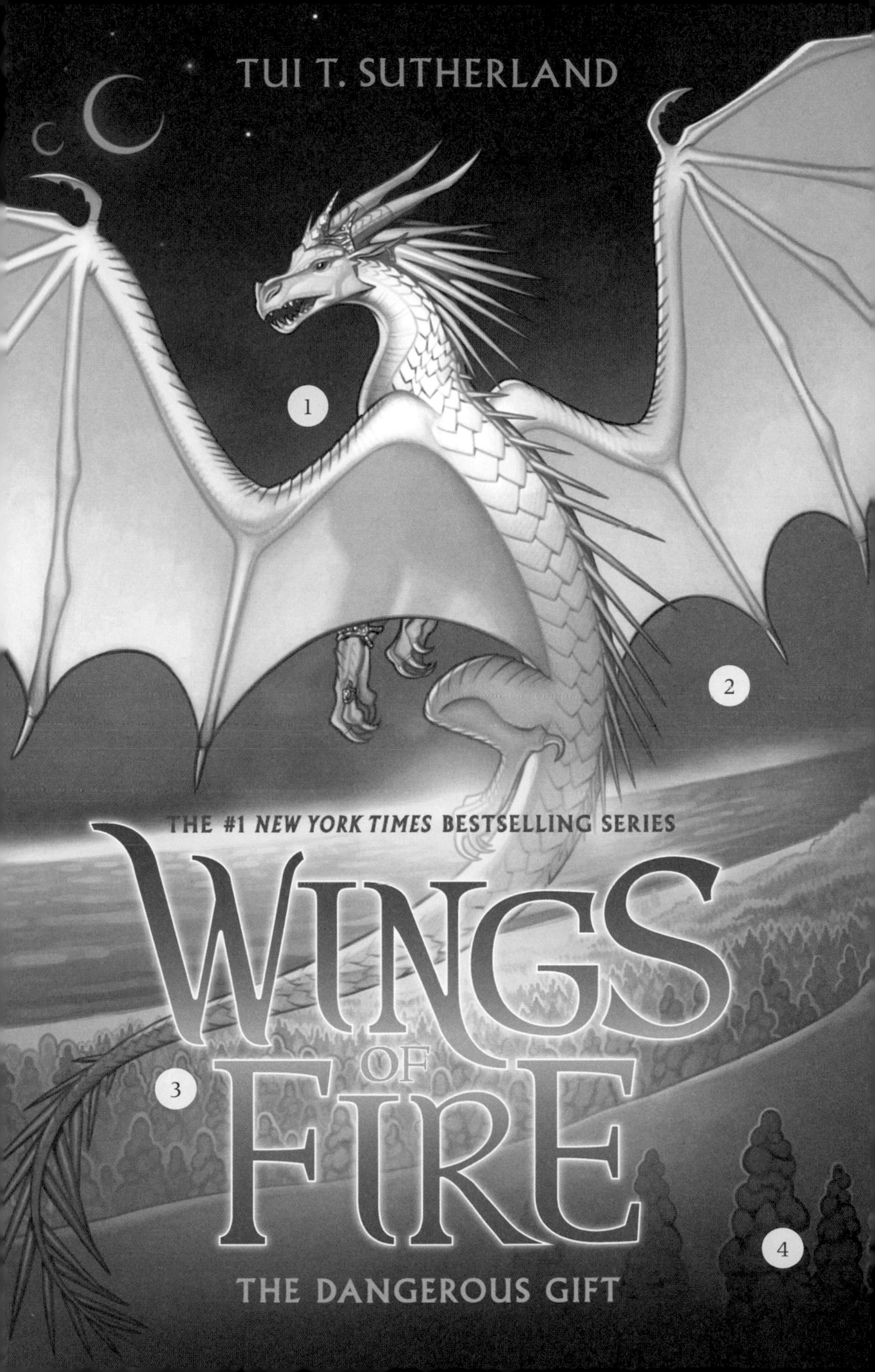

TUI T. SUTHERLAND

THE #1 *NEW YORK TIMES* BESTSELLING SERIES

WINGS
OF
FIRE

THE DANGEROUS GIFT

DRAW YOUR OWN COVER!

Use this page to sketch your cover ideas, and be sure to draw more than one. These sketches can be small and unrefined — they are sketches, after all!

Now that you've had a chance to explore various cover ideas, draw your final cover on this page.

WRITE YOUR BIOGRAPHY

Once you've told your dragons' story, it's time to tell your own!
All your favorite books include biographies for the authors
and artists.

Answer these questions to start writing your own biography.

Where and when were you born?

Where do you live?

Who are the members of your family?

Do you have any pets?

What are your favorite things to do?

What is one fun fact about you?

Turn your answers into a biography! Most biographies are written in third person, using *he/she/they* instead of *I/me*. Peek at the biographies at the back of this book for inspiration!

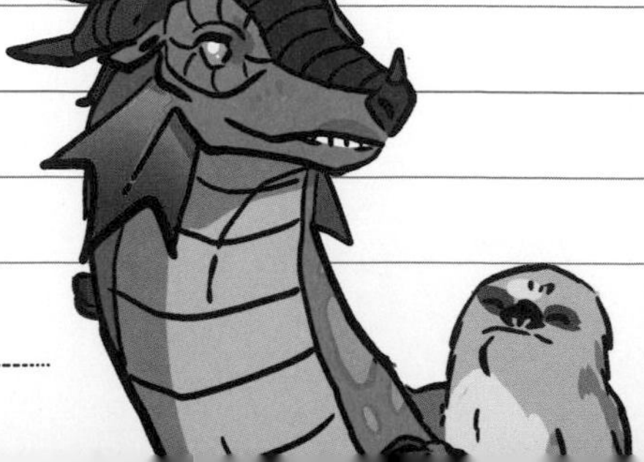

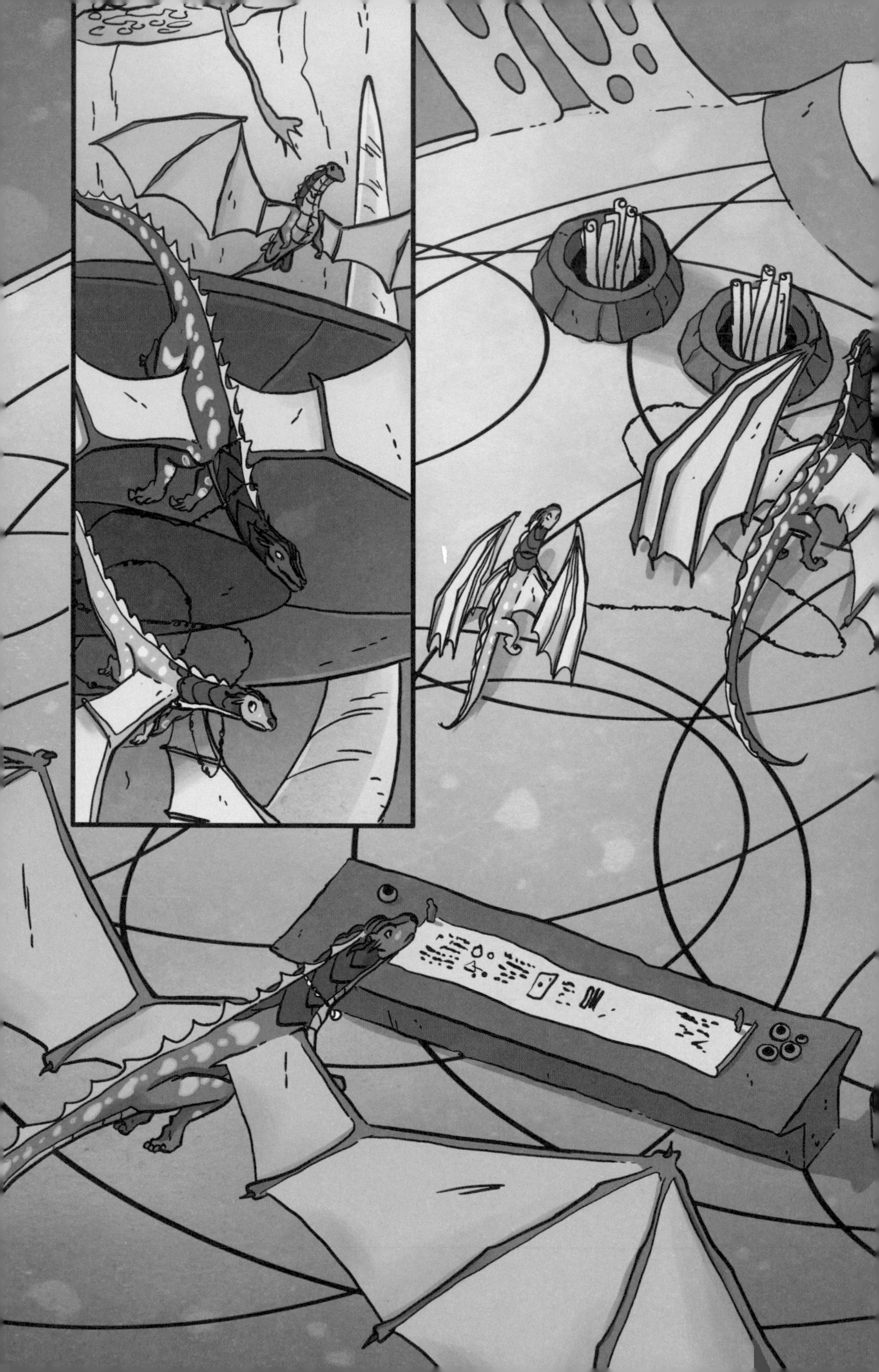

CREATE!

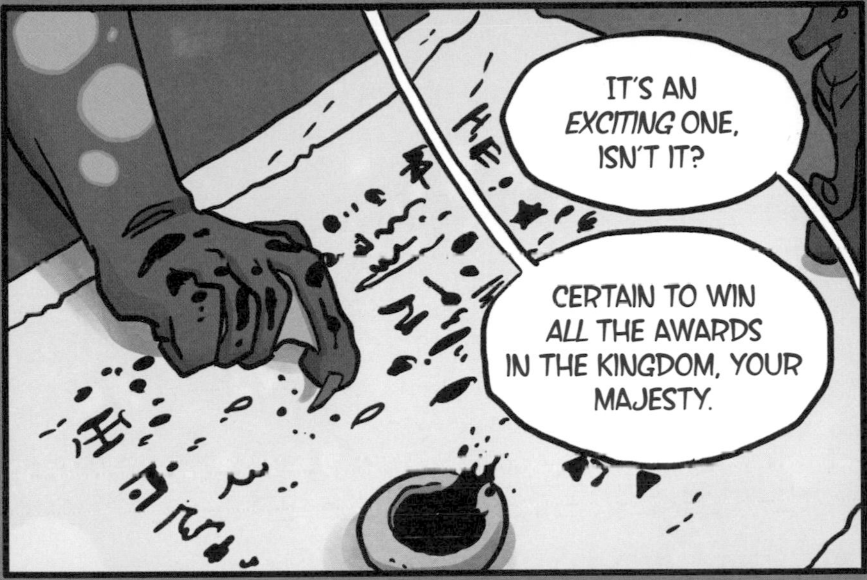
IT'S AN
EXCITING ONE,
ISN'T IT?
CERTAIN TO WIN
ALL THE AWARDS
IN THE KINGDOM, YOUR
MAJESTY.

These last few pages are all for you! Write and draw your story in the way that only you can. Be sure to have some extra paper nearby so you can keep creating after you've filled the pages of this book.

Happy storytelling!

TUI T. SUTHERLAND is the author of the #1 *New York Times* and *USA Today* bestselling Wings of Fire series, the Menagerie trilogy, and the Pet Trouble series, as well as a contributing author to the bestselling Spirit Animals and Seekers series (as part of the Erin Hunter team). In 2009, she was a two-day champion on *Jeopardy!* She lives in Massachusetts with her wonderful husband, two awesome sons, and two very patient dogs. To learn more about Tui's books, visit her online at www.tuibooks.com.

MIKE HOLMES has drawn for the series Secret Coders, Adventure Time, and Bravest Warriors. He created the comic strip True Story, the art project *Mikenesses*, and his work can be seen in *MAD* magazine. He lives in Philadelphia with his wife, Meredith, and son, Oscar, along with Heidi the dog and Ella the cat.

MAARTA LAIHO spends her days and nights as a comic colorist, where her work includes the comics series Lumberjanes, Adventure Time, and The Mighty Zodiac. When she's not doing that, she can be found hoarding houseplants and talking to her cat. She lives in the woods of Maine.